RAVEN

TERESA GABELMAN

The Protectors Series

RAVEN

Copyright 2022 Teresa Gabelman

All rights reserved. The right of Teresa Gabelman to be identified as the author of this work has been asserted in accordance with the Copyright, Designs and Patents Act 1988. This is a work of fiction and any resemblance between the characters and persons living or dead is purely coincidental.

Gabelman, Teresa (2022-7-30). Raven (The Protectors Series) Book #18 Kindle Edition.

❈ Created with Vellum

CHAPTER 1

*R*aven rode toward training, a light rain had begun to fall from the dark heavy clouds above. The day fit her mood...dark and heavy. She had felt that way for weeks. No matter what she did she couldn't shake the feeling of doom looming over her shoulder. Raven practically begged for more shifts, which Sloan granted without question. They were so swamped he took what he could get out of all of his Warriors. Even with the Guardians merging with the Warriors it still seemed they were far outnumbered. Things weren't getting better, they seemed to be getting worse. Human and blood trafficking was at an all-time high, rogues were running rampant and there was an uptick in half-breeds again.

Stopping at a light she reached back grabbing her leather jacket out of the small storage compartment on her bike and quickly put it on just as the light turned green. A car pulled out in front of her making her slide on the wet pavement.

"Watch it asshole!" She yelled as the car continued on its way. She thought about going after the idiot, but figured she was already running late. Plus, she was sure Sloan wouldn't appreciate a call that she had killed someone for running a red light. With her already dark mood she had a feeling that's what would happen, so she used her hard-earned self-control and continued on her way.

A few minutes later she was pulling into the warehouse. Two of the black vans sat in front with all the Warriors and Guardians standing around. As one they all turned to glare her way.

"What the hell?" She whispered to herself as she parked. She was late, but not that late. Getting off the bike she took her jacket off and put it back into the compartment. Turning she looked at Charger who was staring at her, then to Sloan who stood with both hands on his hips with that ready to bitch her out look on his face.

"Before you say anything I'd just like you to know that I was almost hit after some asshole ran a red light and I didn't kill him." Raven figured she'd start with that since Sloan looked pissed.

"Well maybe if you'd been on time, you would have missed the asshole by about…" He glanced at his watch. "fifteen minutes."

Shit, he always had a fucking comeback…a good comeback at that.

"What?" Sloan tilted his head. "No other excuses? Is that all you got?"

"Pretty much." Raven said with a shrug.

"Get in the fucking van." He growled with a nod toward one of the vans parked in front of the warehouse.

"Ah, why? Aren't we having training?" Raven questioned without moving. When Sloan gave her an even deeper glare, she frowned throwing up her hands. "Okay. Okay."

"Still pushing boundaries?" Jared whispered as she passed him.

He may be her father, but she was still pissed at him and Charger. The name Louis Maxwell Jr. blasted through her head sending anger at them both surging to the surface. Ignoring Jared, she climbed into the back of the van and frowned. Katrina, who was the only one that gave her a welcoming smile, along with four other trainees sat in the back all staring at her. Sitting down next to Katrina and across from the four trainees she moved to make room for Jared and Charger. She didn't take her eyes off the guys staring back at her.

Sloan climbed into the back of the van which was surprising then slammed the door. "Hope you guys are ready."

"Ready for what?" Katrina asked what they all were wanting to know.

"You're initiation into the Warriors." Sloan replied giving them each a look. "And you better not embarrass our unit."

"Ah, wait?" One of the guys said, his eyes round with shock and if Raven wasn't mistaken, a tinge of fear. "Are we ready?"

Raven rolled her eyes. "Speak for yourself." Raven snorted. She had been ready. If anything, Raven loved a challenge.

One of the guys, Kent, she thought was his name glared at her, but remained silent.

"So, which one of you assholes are going to take me out?" Raven inquired not at all surprised at the shocked look on their faces. Daniel had finally told her exactly who it was, but she wanted to see if the dick had the balls to admit it. "You?"

"What if it was?" Kent replied breaking his silence.

Okay that wasn't an admission so maybe he just had one ball, she'd give him that since none of the others were looking at her now. Raven slowly leaned toward him, her eyes narrowing and then a slow smile spread across her lips. "Looking forward to you trying." Her voice was low, but everyone heard her words and the challenge behind them.

"Enough!" Sloan growled which sounded like a shout in the back of the enclosed van. "You work as a team, or you will fail."

Raven gave Kent one last smirk before leaning back against the van, her eyes didn't leave his as she responded to Sloan. "I will not fail. And I never said I wouldn't work as a team, but others seem to have a different mindset."

"Jesus, this is going to be a shitshow." Sloan grumbled running his hands over his eyes.

"Everything we do is a shitshow." Jared added with his own smirk.

"Why weren't we notified about the initiation?" Katrina asked sounding worried.

Raven really liked Katrina. She was talented and had an amazing gift with animals, but she had little confidence in herself. Actually, she was too nice which was something Raven never had a problem with. Though she also wanted to know why they hadn't been informed. It would have been nice to have a heads up. She noticed Sloan and Jared glance at each other and knew the answer. They didn't want anyone other than the Warriors to know about the initiation because of what had happened at the last one where many Warriors were murdered.

Sloan looked at each of them before looking back at Katrina. "You all know what happened at the last initiation." Sloan's voice turned hard. "So that should answer your question."

The van became silent as everyone reflected on what was just said. Raven glanced at Charger who was staring at her. She wanted to stare him down, but instead looked away. She needed to focus on what was ahead for her and the rest of the trainees. Sloan was right, they needed to work as a team because if they didn't it would definitely be a shitshow for them, not the Warriors.

If Kent or any other trainee tried something, then she would deal with it then. At least one person had her back. She glanced at Katrina who gave her a nod as if she knew exactly what Raven had been thinking.

"So, uh, what's the rules?" One of the trainees asked his voice cracking with nerves.

Both Jared and Charger chuckled, even Sloan grinned. "Son, there are no rules."

"Survive." Jared shrugged his shoulders looking at all of them. "And make it to the end."

Raven watched the guy visibly swallow. She rolled her eyes again then leaned her head back against the hard metal of the van. Slowly she closed her eyes and cleared her mind. With Charger practically sitting across from her that wasn't easy, but she forced herself to do it. Going into the unknown was something she was used to. Working with Demons for so many years had prepared her to expect anything and everything that was thrown her way. She used that knowledge in her everyday life.

As much as she tried to keep Charger out of her thoughts, she felt his gaze on her. She didn't have to open her eyes to know he was staring at her. That was how well she knew him, and it sucked. She understood his reasoning of wanting to keep his distance to a point. Charger had been keeping Jake from killing himself after losing his mate, Tracy. Her death had devastated them all, but Jake the most. After witnessing what Jake was going through Charger had stepped back from her, keeping her at arm's length. Even though she understood it, that didn't mean the rejection still didn't hurt. Plus thinking on it she could be killed at any moment in her line of work, so wouldn't he want to spend as much time with her as he could if he truly did care. Doubts of his feelings for her surfaced more than she would like, but she just pushed everything away and focused on what needed to be done which included guarding her heart once again and steering clear of Charger.

The ride became bumpy making her eyes snap open. The van slowed then came to an abrupt halt. Sloan opened the door then stepped out as everyone followed. Raven hung back letting everyone go, then noticed Charger had also stayed inside. Once everyone was out, he reached over and closed the van door.

"Some would call this kidnapping." Raven said with a cocked eyebrow.

"Don't be a smartass." He replied with a frown.

"When have I not been a smartass?" Raven shot back then moved forward to reach for the door, but he stopped her.

"That's exactly why you need to watch yourself out there, Raven." Charger warned her. His eyes narrowed slightly. "Not only have you made enemies with some of the trainees, but there are going to be a lot of Warriors here today that you may or may not have pissed off at some time in the past."

Raven sighed knowing the truth of what he just said. Even though the Guardians were not as well known as the Warriors to the everyday society, they had many dealings with each other. Some collabs went smoothly while others not so much. Not that it bothered her, though it did mean she was going to have to watch her back even more now. "Thanks, but I've got this." She said, then moved again to get out of the van and again he stopped her.

"Dammit, Raven." Charger hissed in her face. "I'm fucking serious. Let me finish."

Raven sighed then moved back. "Continue." She flipped her hand in the air in aggravation.

"Guardians that have merged are also here to help." This time it was him who cocked his eyebrow at her.

"Oh, is that so?" Raven replied with a snort. "Some of the ones that called me a traitor?"

"Do you always have to be so…" Charger stopped speaking as he glared at her.

"So…what?" She questioned with a frown. "So…offended by being called a traitor when in fact most of them did the same exact thing I did only a few months later?"

"It's different and you know it." Charger just shook his head with a sigh. "Why are you so combative all the fucking time?"

Okay, that surprised her. She hadn't expected him to say something like that. Did he even know her? Really know her. At least she thought he did, maybe she had been wrong, and he didn't know her at all. "Yeah, Charger and for good fucking reason." Her voice was low, but packed a punch full on attitude. "I've had to fight for every scrap of anything I've gotten in this world."

When he tried to speak, she threw up her hand and stopped him.

"Oh, hell no. You brought it up so let me fucking finish. I thought you knew me, but I guess I was wrong." She added that with narrowed eyes keeping the hurt completely hidden from him. "Combative has not only kept me alive, but sane. I don't give two shits about what anyone thinks of me or what I do, and that includes you. Someone rubs me the wrong way or says something I don't like then yeah, I become combative because that's all I know and I fucking like it that way. So, fuck you and your thoughts."

Charger just sat there and stared at her for a long moment. He finally leaned in close to her, his golden eyes glowing in the darkness. "Let's get one thing straight, Raven." Charger's head tilted slightly. "I know you better than you realize, maybe even more than you know yourself."

She also tilted her head in a mocking manner leaning closer to him, her eyes so narrowed she could barely see him. She felt her fangs grow in anger. "And I call bullshit, Charger McNeil. You know nothing."

"What in the fuck are you doing?" The door slammed open as Sloan glared inside. "Get your ass out here, Raven. Now!"

Raven continued to glare at Charger as she scooted past him then climbed out of the back of the van. More than anyone that man could rile her up to the point she was ready to kill the next person that looked at her sideways. Looking around she saw that they were in a large field surrounded by nothing but thick woods. It was rainy with a hazy fog tipping the tree line.

Glancing around she spotted Kane who gave her a wink then a nod of encouragement. Her eyes then moved from him to look around the field at all the Warriors, Guardians, and trainees. There was a lot of them. Damn if someone wanted to take them out, they sure could without a problem. The secrecy was definitely warranted.

She also noticed some of the Warriors and Guardians were wearing vests. Some had a blue X and others had a white X. Then her eyes caught site of the vests with the red X. That's when Jared tossed one her way. She frowned down at it holding it out.

"I'm not wearing this target?" Raven tossed it back at Jared. "Thanks, but no thanks."

"Wear it or walk the fuck out of here." Sloan growled grabbing the vest from Jared and throwing it back at her. "You want easy, you are in the wrong fucking place. It's meant to be a target." Sloan said loud enough for everyone to hear.

Raven glared at the vest then put it on and zipped it up. This was total bullshit, but she kept that to herself this time.

"If you don't like it, then walk your pussy ass right on out of here." Sloan repeated to the group of trainees who had yet to put their own vests on.

Steve, who must have been in the other van, slowly moved up next to her. "I almost did walk when I had to do this shit on this very field. Flipping burgers sounded mighty fine to me at that time." Steve whispered as Sloan began giving instructions. "After getting disqualified saving Jill's ass and then walking out of the shitter only to get shot in the fucking chest had me rethinking my decision to stay. Watch your ass out there, Raven. This shit is no joke."

Raven glanced over at Steve. She'd heard what had happened at the last initiation. Steve had almost died that day. A lot of Warriors had died that day. Giving Steve a pat on the shoulder she then turned her attention to Sloan deciding to give this initiation the respect it deserved as well as the ones that died on this very same field.

CHAPTER 2

"Can everyone hear me?" Sloan's deep voice boomed across the field. "Because if you can't you are going to have a big problem once that horn blows."

Raven watched as everyone nodded. She noticed all of the Guardians were wearing vests with a white X. She had no clue what the X's stood for, but she figured she was getting ready to find out.

"Many died on the field you are standing on. Most I'm sure have heard about it and I'm not going to repeat it. I had a lot of push back about having the initiation here, but I know the Warriors that gave their lives that day wouldn't want it any other way. It's where initiations have been held for centuries. So here we are."

All the Warriors thumped their chests in sync out of respect for their fallen.

"You will be in teams of four. All Guardians are wearing vests with a white X and will be paired with a Warrior is also wearing a white X. No Guardian who has merged will have to go through the initiation process." Sloan then glanced at Raven. "Unless they fully switched to our side."

Raven felt all eyes fall on her, but she ignored it keeping her own eyes on Sloan. Fuck them if they thought she was a traitor.

"Anyone you see with a white X is an observer. If an observer says you are out, then you are out. Is that understood?" Sloan eyed the crowd then nodded when everyone shouted their understanding. "Anyone with a blue X is a hunter. I think that is self-explanatory. You see a blue X then know your time is numbered. Slade is the only medic." Sloan nodded toward Slade who raised his hand in the air for anyone who didn't know him.

"I have helpers that will be around. Anyone with a black baseball hat like myself is considered a medic and if they can't handle the issue, they will contact me." Slade called out getting nods of understanding from the crowd.

"As for the rules, there are no rules. Each team will be given a map to the end point locations, one paintball gun with limited ammunition. So make your shots count. All Hunters will have bright yellow paintballs. We have no half-breeds this time so all shots count because all paintballs will be considered as silver bullets. Trainees will have bright red paintballs. You shoot a hunter then they are also out. I highly suggest you shoot any hunter you see because they are going to outnumber you."

"Good luck with that." A Warrior Raven didn't know snorted then glanced straight at her. She memorized his face and build because he was sure as hell going down if she got the chance.

"Any questions so far?" Sloan asked, then continued when no one said anything. "Good. The course is five miles. You must make it to your first location which is on the map, make sure an observer sees you there and then make it back here within the time period of one hour. You will hear a horn that will sound in ten minutes. That is telling you trainees to get your asses moving. You will have only five minutes before a second horn will sound. That horn indicates the hunters are going to be up your asses. The last horn you will hear means the end of the initiation. If you haven't made it back here by that time, then you have failed. If at any time you hear the horn blow with a consistency that means something has happened and to get back here as fast as you can."

Murmurs filled the field, but Raven wasn't worried. An hour was fine with her.

"An hour?" Katrina sighed beside her. "I don't know if I'm ready for this."

Raven frowned then looked at Katrina. "You are more ready than any of these assholes." She nodded toward Kent and the rest of them who all stood together. "I'm going to make sure we are on the same team. Don't worry. We got this, Katrina."

Katrina nodded looking a little more confident.

"Okay get with your leaders and split into your teams. They will give your team the confidential word. If anyone on the team tells a hunter your confidential word your whole team not only fails, but will be banned from participating in an initiation for more than a year. Now get with your team." Sloan ordered, then turned toward Jared and Sid who had been in the other van with the other four trainees.

Blaze walked over toward Katrina wearing a vest with a blue X. "Oh, no." Katrina said with wide eyes. "You're a hunter?"

He pulled her in his arms and gave her a kiss on the forehead. "I am, but not against our unit. We don't hunt our own."

"Wouldn't matter." Raven grinned up at him. "I'd take him out before he could even get to us."

"That confident, are we?" Blaze chuckled when she nodded. "Good. You're going to need that confidence when the horn blows."

Raven saw the worry in Blaze's eyes as he looked from her back to Katrina. She briefly wondered what it would feel like to have someone care that much about her. Her eyes wanted to go to Charger, but she refused to let them.

"Watch yourself out there Katrina." Blaze whispered, but Raven heard him say, "*I love you.*"

Katrina nodded giving him a brave smile. "I love you." She repeated his words back to him.

"Okay, I'm going to puke." Raven said, then pulled Katrina away from Blaze. "Go on. Get. I've got to make sure my girl is ready. Don't you worry about her, she's got this."

"We have an odd number." Jared said with Charger, Sid, and Sloan behind him.

"We've got our teams. Us four and them." Kent said then looked at Raven with a smirk. "Guess you ladies will have to wait until next time."

"Hey dipshit." Jared growled at Kent. "Who the fuck made you boss?"

"It's fine." Raven said without worry. "Me and Katrina are a team. Just give us our word and the map."

"What?" Charger and Jared said at the same time.

"Yeah." Katrina frowned at her. "What?"

Raven glanced at Sloan. "Is there a rule on the number in the team? Oh, wait. You said no rules, so I guess we're good."

"There can't be more than four to a team." Sloan informed her with a frown.

"Well, good since that's not the problem." Raven responded knowing she was probably pushing it with Sloan, but just couldn't seem to stop herself. "And honestly if the eight little bitch boys want to team up together, I'm fine with it."

"Hey, bitch." Kent growled taking a step toward her, but Charger cut him off.

"You best step back before I disqualify you right now." Charger snarled leaning over the guy.

"Let me see if any other unit has an odd number." Sid took off at a jog.

"I'm going to say this once." Sloan pointed at Kent then the rest of the trainees. "We are a fucking unit. Just because you are on a different team doesn't mean you don't help each other out. If I hear that one of you assholes try to hurt the other team in my unit I will personally hurt you. Is that understood?"

"Yes, sir." All eight of them said in unison.

Sloan turned toward Raven. "That goes for you also."

"I'm not the one with the problem." Raven said, then glared at Kent.

"I'll be on their team." Daniel walked up with Duncan beside him. He glanced at Sloan. "Sorry I'm a little late."

"This ought to be good. Two females and a freak." Kent smirked at his friends, but none of them smirked back.

Raven saw red as she headed toward the asshole to rip his face off, but Daniel stopped her with a shake of his head. "Save it for the initiation."

It took everything she had not to tear Kent's smirk off his face, but Daniel was right. She needed to chill out before Sloan killed her and she fucked up the initiation for all of them. She would let it go for now. The bastard could say whatever he wanted about her, but when he said shit about people she cared about that's where she drew the line.

"You sure you're ready?" Sloan frowned at Daniel, then glanced toward Duncan who didn't say a word.

"I'm ready." Daniel gave him a confident nod.

"He's ready." Raven added for good measure backing Daniel up. She had seen the kid train and he was more ready than any of them.

"Found one." Sid said as he walked up with the skinniest vampire Raven had ever seen. She would bet her last dollar that this dude in his human life had been a nerd.

"I thought we had to team with our unit." Raven said, not really wanting to hurt this guy's feelings, but shit she also didn't need to carry someone through the initiation. "Plus, Daniel showed up and is teaming with us."

"He's from Columbus so close enough." Sid said with a grin knowing what she was thinking. "And with Daniel that gives you four like everyone else."

"I'm Stanley." He held out his small hand toward her.

"I'm Raven." She said shaking his fragile looking hand. Raven definitely would have guessed this dude's name. She heard Kent and the others snicker but ignored them. "I'm Raven. This is Katrina and Daniel. You ready to kick some ass?"

"Ah, sure." He said with a nod, looking scared to death.

Jared walked over with Steve following waving them closer to him. "Your word is…" Jared grinned as he looked at them. "Antballs."

"Yes!" Steve did a fist pump.

"Huh?" Stanley frowned as did Raven and Katrina while Daniel just chuckled. "Antballs?"

"Yeah, you see…" Steve started, but Adam had walked up and grabbed Steve by the back of the neck.

"Don't ask." Adam pulled Steve away with Jared laughing.

"Yeah, don't ask." Jared was still chuckling.

"I don't think antballs will work." Stanley started rubbing his hands together nervously.

"Dude, chill the fuck out." Jared sighed shaking his head. "It could be anything. It doesn't matter. What does matter is you not squealing the word to a hunter like a little bitch."

Raven rolled her eyes at the word then actually smiled at how excited Steve was. One day she would have to ask about antballs, but right now she had more important things to worry about. Her gaze went to Stanley who was freaking the fuck out over a damn word. Okay, this wasn't good, but it was all Raven had to work with. Glancing at Charger she noticed he was staring at Stanley, then his eyes met hers. "I know I'm just wasting my breath, but you could wait until the next initiation."

"You're right." Raven said not losing her gaze with him. "You're wasting your breath."

"Good luck today." Jackson Riley walked up giving her a hug not caring that Charger was right there.

"What are you doing here?" Raven hugged him back. "Come to cheer me on?"

"I wouldn't miss seeing you kick everyone's ass, but I'm also here with the Kentucky Warrior unit we merged with." Jackson smiled down at her.

Damn he was a handsome son of a bitch. Why in the hell couldn't she have feelings for this Dark Guardian instead of grump ass over there glaring at them? "Well, I hate to tell you this, but your unit has no chance. You might want to send them on home."

He turned serious as his smile slipped. "Watch yourself out there, Raven."

She was actually getting tired of hearing everyone say that. "The word traitor still floating around out there?" She glanced across the field at the Guardians who were standing about. A few looked at her, then away quickly.

"We're a tight group and even though most of us merged with the Warriors only you went as far as to transfer completely." Jackson said as if in warning. "Just watch yourself."

Raven nodded then watched him walk away. Her eyes did one more scan of the field and narrowed at any Guardian giving her a look. That was her warning to them.

"So, you'll listen to Riley, but not me?" Charger said as he walked closer.

"He doesn't piss me off." Raven shrugged being honest. It was true. Charger pissed her off. Jackson didn't.

Charger sighed running his hand down his face in aggravation. "Listen, the kid doesn't have any real gift that I'm picking up." He informed her. Charger's gift was knowing what gifts others had. It was a strange gift but came in handy. "But Adam read him and he's smart."

"He's a nerd. Of course, he's smart." Raven looked over at Adam who was scanning the field. "Didn't need Adam to tell me that."

"Give him the map. You focus on keeping your asses safe and getting to the end goal." Charger ordered and yep, it pissed her off.

"I already planned on giving Stan the map." Raven growled then glared up at him. "You know Charger, you go months without hardly saying a word to me except in the cemetery about why you can't be around me, which I heard loud and clear as well as understand. I've done my best to stay away from you, so I think maybe you need to do the same because I know what I'm doing."

She saw hurt flash across his eyes before he narrowed them at her. God she was such a bitch.

"Watch your ass." He said as he pointed at her then turned to walk away.

"You got a game plan with your team?" Jared walked up holding out the map just as Charger stomped away. He must have realized she didn't by the look on her face. "What in the fuck have you been doing the past ten minutes? Get your head out of your ass, Raven. This is fucking serious."

"Shit." Raven snatched the map out of his hand just as the horn blew.

CHAPTER 3

Raven and Katrina quickly looked at each other as all the trainees took off at a run. Within seconds they were following them into the dense forest. She glanced behind her to see Stanley just standing there looking around in confusion. Turning she rushed back, grabbed his arm, and dragged him with her. Catching up to Katrina and Daniel who waited at the edge, Raven led the way. They had five minutes before the hunters were set loose. Fuck, they needed a plan.

"Stan." Raven said as they stopped. She shoved the map at him. "Your job is to lead us where we need to go. Our job is to keep you from getting disqualified or killed."

"My name's Stanley." He said as if in a fog of confusion.

"Yeah, well, I'm calling you Stan." Raven looked around then back at him. "The girls will love it. You can thank me later. Right now, we need to get going. Look at the fucking map and tell us which way to go."

"You really think the girls will like it?" His eyes widened as he looked up from the map.

Raven glared down at him. "Dude, you really don't want to piss me off because I will be the one to disqualify you and I don't have the right color paintballs."

Stanley swallowed visibly knowing the only other way to disqualify him would be death. He glanced quickly down at the map again, then looked around. Raven also looked around trying to calm the frantic energy racing through her body. Seeing movement, she looked over to see Kent and his team moving past them. He glanced her way with a large smirk. She flipped him off.

"The best way to go would be north-east and then—" Stanley began but Raven grabbed him and pushed him slightly.

"Just go." Raven hated to be like that…okay, she didn't really, but dammit they were running out of time. "Lead the way and make it fast."

Raven, Daniel, and Katrina kept their eyes peeled for any movement as they rushed toward their first location. The horn sounded indicating the hunters were heading into the forest now. Dammit, that was a short five fucking minutes.

Stanley stopped looking in a direction then quickly took off that way. "I wish I knew where in the hell we were. Are we in Ohio or Kentucky?"

Raven shushed him. "Be quiet." She whispered as they made their way deeper into the wooded area. She made sure they stayed in the shadows of the trees and bushes. "Why does that matter?" Raven asked because honestly, she didn't know. There were no windows in the van, and she couldn't remember if she had ever known the true location of the initiations since she had been a Dark Guardian.

"Well, I guess it doesn't really matter. I mean Kentucky has cave systems and more mountains. Ohio is flatter. I just really don't want to walk off a cliff." Stanley said glancing down at the map again.

"You're a vampire. You'll probably live." Raven hissed, then grabbed both Katrina and Stanley pulling them down behind some brush. Daniel was already kneeling his head cocked listening.

"Kentucky." Daniel said quietly.

"Huh?" Stanley wrinkled his nose as he stared at Daniel's odd swirling eyes.

"We're in Kentucky." Daniel glanced behind them. "Now shut the fuck up."

"Did you hear something?" A male voice asked from close behind them. "I swear I heard someone talking."

Two skunks scurried past ignoring them. Raven glanced at Stanley whose eyes were wide as saucers. He started to open his mouth, but she clamped her hand over his mouth shaking her head at him.

Raven glanced at Katrina who gave her a wink as they all four remained rooted to their spots. She tried to estimate exactly where the men were, but she wasn't sure. Dammit they should be further than they were. She refused to fail.

"Holy shit." A man shouted. They were very close. "Watch it!"

"What in the hell are they doing?" Another hunter's voice shouted. "Oh, hell no. They are turning around with their tails raised. Fuck this shit. I'm out of here."

Raven grinned when she heard them take off loudly in the opposite direction. She glanced at Katrina who had her hand over her own mouth laughing. "Good job." She whispered, then removed her hand from Stanley's mouth. "Come on we have to get going. Keep talking to a minimum."

Both Katrina and Stanley nodded as they took off keeping low and hidden as they raced toward their destination. Suddenly Katrina skidded to a stop, but her feet slid underneath a large bush just as her body started to disappear. Daniel dove and grabbed her wrist just as she was heading over a large cliff. Raven helped Daniel pull her up, then glanced down at the deep crevice.

"Definitely in Kentucky." Stanley whispered more to himself as he also looked over the edge.

Raven nudged him along after making sure Katrina was okay. After a while Raven realized that something just didn't feel right. They only had one close call. If the hunters outnumbered them then why hadn't they been everywhere. Either something was definitely up, or these Warriors sucked. She knew that wasn't the case so that meant her instincts were right. Something wasn't adding up. Katrina threw up her hand motioning for them to stop as they all four knelt.

The sound of popping paintball guns reached their ears. "The location is right over the ridge. Looks like a clearing of some sort on the map." Stanley whispered.

"You thinking what I'm thinking?" Daniel frowned over at her.

She knew Daniel had certain powers, but no one knew what they were. She nodded at him. "Unfortunately, I think so." Raven replied glancing at him. "You didn't see this coming I take it?"

Daniel actually grinned even during their dire circumstances. "Now what fun would that be?"

Raven snorted then cursed realizing she knew exactly what was over that ridge and so did Daniel. Every hunter was over that ridge protecting the observer they had to check in with. And by the sound of it not many trainees were being successful. Suddenly some deer came out of the trees and surrounded them as the woods became loud with the sound of birds. Katrina was giving them protection and security.

"What are we going to do?" Katrina frowned and Raven realized she also figured out what was going on.

"I don't know." Raven sighed with a curse. "Dammit, I wish I could see what was going on and where the observer was. That would be a start."

"Coming right up." Katrina said just as a beautiful hawk flew toward them landing on Katrina's outstretched arm. Raven watched as Katrina stared into the bird's eyes before she lifted her arm, and it flew off.

"Okay, are you like Dr. Doolittle or something?" Stanley whispered his eyes still round as saucers and Raven wondered if they were going to permanently be stuck that way after this ordeal.

"Something like that." Katrina smiled with a nod. It wasn't long after that the hawk came back. Again Katrina stared at it, tilting her head sideways as she appeared to communicate silently with the magnificent bird. Within minutes she lifted her arm, and the hawk once again took off. "Give me the map."

Stanley handed it over and Katrina stared at it as more paintball shots reached them. Guess when Sloan said there were no rules, he meant it. Seemed pretty petty for the big bad Warrior hunters to gather where they had to check in. Lazy asses are what they were, and she definitely wouldn't call them hunters.

"Right here is where the check-in observer is." Katrina pointed then ran her finger along the outline of the forest. "And this is where all the hunters are."

"Isn't that cheating?" Stanley frowned staring at the map.

"Not if there aren't any rules." Daniel reminded him.

"You can look at it one of two ways." Raven stared at the map. "It's either very smart or just plain cockiness with a side of laziness."

"I really don't want to have to repeat this." Katrina frowned. "And I hate cocky ass people."

"Yeah, so do I." Raven looked around then stood. "That's why we are going to succeed in this fucking thing. Okay, here's the plan."

"We got a plan?" Stanley said looking at his watch.

"I always have a plan." Raven knelt back down. "Most of them are pretty good and usually work out."

There went Stanley's eyes again, wide as saucers. "Pretty good and *usually* work? That doesn't sound promising."

"Nothing in life is promising, Stan." Raven snorted then put the map down on the ground between them. "From this map it looks like there is a trail of some sort going around the clearing. If I can get around this and come in from the back, I can make contact with the observer before any of the hunters see me."

"But what if there are hunters along the path?" Stanley said with a frown. "What then?"

"Then I'll take them out." Raven replied without hesitation.

"By yourself?" Stanley's eyes started to widen again, but Raven ignored him.

"Daniel, you need to give me a little bit of time to get myself in place." Raven looked at Daniel hoping this plan worked. She was wanting to see some sort of confidence in his gaze, but his swirling eyes showed her nothing. Raven wasn't lying when she said she had good plans, but good plans could turn to shit in a heartbeat. "And then I want you to cause a distraction. Do you think you can do that?"

"In Steve's words…does a bear shit in the woods?" Daniel gave her a half grin this time full of confidence.

"Ah, yes, they do." Stanley answered as if it was a real question.

"I can call on a few friends to help with the distraction." Katrina's smile was a little evil and made Raven proud. "But how are we to know when?"

Raven frowned glancing over at Stanley who was biting his fingernails. "Stan, I want you to open yourself up. When you hear the word *now* in your mind give Daniel and Katrina the signal. Once all hell breaks loose, I want you to run like your life depends on it. We will catch up. Do you think you can find your way back without the map?"

Stanley looked around then nodded. "Yeah, I can."

"Good." Raven gave him a proud nod. "Katrina once it gets to be too much, I want you to run like your ass is on fire. You hear me? I will be right behind you. You too Daniel."

"I'm not leaving you behind, Raven." Daniel said stubbornly. The grin was totally wiped from his face.

"Neither will I." Katrina added. "Don't worry about us. We'll be fine just get yourself back here as soon as you can."

"Ah, so do I still run like my life depends on it?" Stanley asked, his voice shaking slightly.

"Yes!" All three of them said instantly.

Raven then looked at each of them. "This is going to work." She said, then stood and took off hoping her words rung true because honestly, she had her doubts. They were going against seasoned Warriors, and she was the only one out of the three that had any experience with what was about to go down. "Please let this work." She whispered to herself.

A shadow passed overhead causing her to look up. Katrina's hawk was flying a little ahead of her as if showing her the way. Raven smiled. Once this was over and they succeeded she was going to give Katrina the biggest hug and she was definitely not a hugger. The overgrown path began to climb and become a little more treacherous, but Raven continued. She knew she had to be close. Keeping her eyes on the ground and the hawk's shadow she continued. It wasn't until she came to a small decline and bend in the path that the hawk screeched out a long cry as it circled. Not sure what that meant she slowed to a stop and squatted. She was either very close or danger was just ahead, she just didn't know which.

Slowly she moved forward still in a squatted position. There around the bend stood a hunter with a blue X on his vest. His back was to her. Pulling her paintball gun, she frowned afraid that if she shot it the noise would alert not only him but others in the area. He needed to be taken care of as quietly as possible and there was one way that would do the trick. Setting her paintball gun on the ground she slowly stood and made her move. Thankfully she and the hunter were pretty much the same height. At least something was on her side.

With lightning speed, she attacked from the back slipping her arm quickly underneath his chin. She sucked him in so close to her chest she could feel the hair on his head tickling her chin as she tightened down on a rear-naked choke. Her surprise attack helped her sink the choke in deep. Feeling his body going limp she slowly walked back loosening her grip on his neck once she knew he was out and dragged him off the trail. By the time he woke up she'd be long gone.

Even though there were no rules she took a paintball from her vest pocket and smashed it against his vest so everyone would know he was out and not in the rear-naked choke way. With a grin she glanced up at the hawk who seemed to be waiting on her. Honestly in the moment she had never really been jealous of anyone, but right now she was jealous of Katrina's powers.

Following the hawk she made her way down the hill, her eyes scanning the area for more hunters, but she didn't see any. Heading toward the rock she knelt behind it and looked around. The hawk circled over an area and that's when she spotted the observer she needed to make it to. She also saw all the hunters standing around as if they didn't have a care in the world. Honestly, it pissed her off. With narrowed eyes it was time to put her plan to the test and she hoped to hell it worked because these assholes needed to learn a lesson and that lesson was…women fucking ruled.

CHAPTER 4

Raven did one more scan around the area and hoped Daniel and Katrina were prepared. It was now or never. Opening her mind, she let go of the word *now* hoping that Stanley didn't fuck this up. She did it once more just in case. Raven watched the far end of the field waiting. Shit, did they get caught? Other plans started to form in her head just in case, but suddenly stopped as Katrina stepped out of the woods surrounded by at least fifty coyotes. Damn, this girl and her coyotes. Where in the hell did they all come from and where in the hell was Daniel? Her eyes scanned the area, but she didn't see him. She glanced at the Hunters. None of them were aware yet.

"What the fuck?" A hunter not far from her saw Katrina and aimed his paintball gun. "We got one boys and she has company."

Murmurs from the hunters filled the air as they all stared at the sight of little Katrina surrounded by ferocious looking coyotes. They all aimed their weapons at her, but she didn't even flinch.

"Give us your confidential word and you won't be shot." One hunter said who stood closest to Katrina.

"I don't think so. I need to speak to the observer." Katrina's voice rang across the field. "So, if you'll excuse me."

Laughter filled the air as Katrina took a step, the coyotes surrounding her. Okay, Raven had to give it to Katrina. She had a set of balls on her. Facing down all these Warriors with not one ounce of fear on her face. Holy shit. She looked around to see if Blaze was in the crowd but didn't see him anywhere. He definitely would be proud of his Mate. Damn, she needed to make her move, but had a feeling something big was about to happen and she really needed to wait.

"Girl, those coyotes are not going to shield you." Another hunter called out. "Give up your confidential word or prepare to be disqualified."

"I'm not giving up my word." Katrina's voice rose just as the sky darkened and a deafening noise began to fill the field.

Raven looked up to see hundreds of birds cover the greying sky turning it to black and the field looked as if it was midnight. Holy shit this was perfect. Damn Katrina deserved dinner and a hug. Hearing a noise behind her she turned ready to attack but saw Daniel giving her the quiet sign.

"What are you doing?" She mouthed the words at him.

Daniel made his way closer then leaned in close. "You had your friends sneaking up on you." He whispered, then grinned. "Kent and his…buddies are no longer a threat."

"What did you do?" She whispered back with wide eyes.

Daniel's grin grew larger, then he nodded toward the observer without saying another word. Giving him one last narrowed look, she turned making sure her gun was loaded with paintballs then made her way toward the observer. All the hunters had headed toward Katrina giving Raven a clear path.

"Son of a bitch." The observer was saying as she stood behind him unseen.

Glancing up she watched as one of the hunters fired at Katrina and as one the birds headed toward her to protect, but it was the hawk that caught the paintball and crushed it with his talons. The birds swarmed Katrina and the coyotes spread apart, some were seen some were not.

"Holy shit." Raven whispered causing the observer to jump.

"You scared the fuck out of me." He said then relaxed with a grin. "Damn, you sure got them on this one. So far no one has gotten through."

Raven smiled with a shrug. "None of them were women."

"Point taken." He laughed with a nod. "Raven, isn't it?"

"Yes sir." She smiled proudly looking down to see Katrina's mass of birds slowly backing up.

"Noted." The observer said, then frowned. "But you aren't finished yet. You still have to get back to the finish line and I suggest you get your ass moving. These Warriors don't like to be fooled and they will figure out a way to get your girl down there. Is that Blaze's mate? Heard about her power. Pretty fucking cool."

"Yeah." Raven said, then frowned when the Warriors began shooting the birds with paintballs. Katrina wasn't going to like that. Shit. She'd rather take a bullet than see any of her animals get hurt. The birds began to panic, but held their ground. She knew it wouldn't be long before Katrina released them.

Glancing around she saw another boulder at the edge of the field. She took off, got in position behind it and then took aim at the ones shooting the birds. She glanced back at where she had left Daniel only to see him aiming also. Within seconds she took out three hunters as Daniel took out a couple more. A few that were around them were now hunting her and Daniel. They didn't know where the shots had come from.

"Someone is shooting!" A hunter warned, his voice echoing loudly throughout the field.

Raven stayed hidden but peeked to see Katrina take off as the wall of birds separated her from the hunters. She knew now was their chance to go. With everything she had she flew from the boulder toward the heavy wooded area behind her. Paintballs whizzed by her, but she was quicker. Running through thick brush she felt the stinging in her face as it was slapped with limbs and who knew what else. Her body was taking a beating, but she didn't give up.

"This way!" Daniel ordered and she followed.

Raven's eyes spotted Kent and his team of three knocked out leaning against a tree. Daniel ran straight past them then glanced back at her with a shrug. "Better them than us."

Even though she had an idea these assholes were trying to sabotage her, and Daniel had stopped them she didn't want them to go out this way. She would be blamed. She quickly knelt and smacked Kent in the face, maybe a little harder than needed, but it did the trick. He woke up in a panic, his wide eyes focusing in on her.

"Hunters about five steps behind me." Was all she said before she once again took off. There, she had done her nice deed for the…year. Within seconds she heard the sound of paintball guns and yelling indicating that her warning had done no good.

"Over here!" Katrina's voice carried to her.

Not slowing she turned and looked to her side to see Katrina running just as fast. Maneuvering herself toward Katrina she chanced a glance behind her. The hunters were gaining ground. She remembered not far up there was another cliff and at the bottom what looked like a river or maybe a lake. Honestly, she hadn't paid that much attention, only that it was there.

"I have to release the birds." Katrina's voice wavered once she got beside her.

"Hold them a little longer." Raven said as she glanced over her shoulder at the wall of birds, then looked over at Katrina. "You trust me?"

Katrina glanced her way almost stumbling but kept her footing. "Yes." She answered without hesitation.

"Good, keep up and keep those birds there for just a little bit longer." Raven ordered as she swerved toward her left. She saw the tree that was split down the middle, probably by lightning and rushed that way. The edge of the cliff came into sight, and she knew that Katrina saw it also because she slowed slightly. Reacting quickly, she grabbed Katrina's hand forcing her the rest of the way just as their feet hit solid air.

Katrina screamed just as the birds stopped in midflight then scattered as one into the sky. She hoped that Daniel had made it, but her concern over Katrina had taken all of her focus.

Raven's grip on Katrina's hand slipped as they made contact with the water. It felt like she hit a brick wall. Her scream ripped under the water, and she thought for a split second she was going to pass out, but fear for Katrina kept her conscious. Kicking upward she broke the surface and immediately scanned for Katrina.

"Over here!" Katrina's voice reached her, and Raven sighed in relief. Making her way quickly toward Katrina she glanced up to see the hunters staring down at them. Some shaking their heads while others raised their paintball guns at them. "Shit. Where's Daniel?"

Katrina didn't answer, but as Raven looked up again Daniel was at the edge of the cliff hidden behind a cluster of bushes. He gave her a thumbs up and then stood gaining the attention of the Hunters. She knew that some of them would follow Daniel, but they would split, and the other half would be on her and Katrina. At least that's what *she* would do.

Reaching Katrina, they swam quickly to the bank. Pulling themselves out Katrina cried in pain. "What's wrong?" Raven looked at her with a frown.

"I don't know." Katrina tried to take a step, but her leg buckled underneath her. "I'm fine. Just go. I'll catch up."

"Fuck that." Raven pulled out the map, but it was ruined from the water. "Shit. The map is no good." The cry of a hawk sounded above them causing Raven to look up.

"Don't need the map." Katrina said as she tried to walk on her leg as she looked toward the cliff where the hunters had disappeared. "But I'm not going to make it. They are going to be here any minute. We don't have much time. Just go and I'll do everything I can to slow them down."

"Yeah, that isn't going to happen." Raven dropped the map. "Get on my back."

"What?" Katrina gasped then shook her head. "No, I'll just slow you down."

"Get on my fucking back or I am going to knock you out then carry you to the finish. We are doing this together or not at all, dammit." Raven glared at her. "Hopefully Stan is already there waiting for us with some cold beers. At least half the Hunters are after Daniel. We have a chance and dammit we are going to make it." Stan better be there, or she was going to kick his nerdy ass for not listening and running his ass off when shit hit the fan.

Both women looked at each other as they heard noise behind them. "That's not animals." Katrina jumped on her back. "Go. I'll do my best to hold them back."

Raven didn't know what she meant by that but figured she was going to send her animal friends to help them out once again. She didn't care as long as they made it. Right now, that was all that mattered.

She followed the shadow of the hawk and when she lost the shadow Katrina directed her on where to go. Thankfully Katrina was small, so her weight only slowed her down slightly. Being a vampire had many benefits and being able to carry another person while running at high-speed while being chased by pissed off Warriors was definitely one of them.

Catching movement out of the corner of her eye she saw Stanley running toward them. "Where the hell have you been?" He said as he kept up running side by side. "And why are you carrying Katrina? Why are you wet?"

"Stan!" Raven huffed as she pushed herself harder than she had ever pushed herself before.

"Yeah?" Stanley said glancing over at her, then back to where they were going.

"Shut the fuck up." Raven ordered. "How far are we?"

"Just past that tree line up ahead." Stanley pointed then gasped. "Oh, no. Watch out!"

"Dammit!" Raven braced herself for a barrage of paintballs. "They circled us." She scanned the area to look for a way but could only see failure and it pissed her off. She hated to fail at anything. The end of the tree line was right there, so close and yet so far away as the hunters once again began raising their paintball guns. She could see the opening, the field and those watching beyond. The hunters were lined up outside the forest as if waiting for them to go through the gauntlet.

Raven eyes scanned looking for Daniel. A slight movement caught her attention and she saw him sneaking toward the line. She knew he could make it, but when his swirling eyes met her a whisper inside her head said, *if you don't make it neither will I."*

"*Yeah, fuck that.*" Was her response and she knew some of the Warriors were reading them as snickers filled her mind. The fuckers thought they had won.

"Give us your confidential word or be disqualified." A hunter yelled as they reached them. It was better bragging rights if the hunters could get your confidential word. Using their paintball guns was the last resort. One thing Jared had repeatedly told her during training was never give your word no matter what. It was better to go down in the blaze of paintball glory than give your confidential word. It meant that you could be trusted within the Warrior world. Made sense.

Raven didn't slow down, but saw Stanley open his mouth. "If you say one word, I will kill you."

She knew the hunters were thinking they won and maybe they did, but she'd be damned if she would lay down. She would fight until the very end. Hearing clicking sounds she knew they were about to be pelted with paintballs. Her eyes scanned the finish and what she saw almost made her stumble. Jake stood by Charger as they watched and for some reason seeing Jake made her more determined. For the first time since Tracy's death, she saw something other than sorrow in his eyes as he looked at her. Tracy's image floated through her mind… *'don't you dare give up!'*

"Katrina, we need a little help." Raven said just as the hawk swooped past them heading toward one of the hunters. Suddenly curses filled the air as small and large animals came out of nowhere distracting the hunters once again.

"Working on it." Katrina yelled as she was being jarred on Raven's back. They broke through the woods and only had a few more yards to go. Paintballs whizzed by them, but because of the animals they were wild shots. Honestly, she didn't know if they were shooting at the animals or them at this point. She didn't care. Suddenly the sound of flapping hit her ears and hundreds of birds once again lined them on each side giving them a clear shot at the finish line.

Victory was so close she could taste it. Only a few more…

"Jump!" Katrina screamed interrupting her thoughts just as a hunter ran in front of them with his paintball raised straight at her.

Raven jumped leaping over the hunter's head, then heard a yell behind her. She and Katrina hit the ground hard, sliding for what seemed like forever. She finally came to a stop on her back as the horn sounded. Lifting her head, she saw Daniel pushing off the Hunter as he made his way toward them. Her head fell back against the ground. They had made it.

"I am never doing that again." Stanley moaned as he slowly stood up. "Ever."

Raven looked from Stan to Daniel who stood with a huge grin then to Katrina who also lay on her back.

Katrina slowly turned her head to look at Raven and began laughing. "You did it." Katrina smiled brightly at her.

"No." Raven shook her head, then sat up. "*We* fucking did it. You, Daniel, Stan and me."

It had been a very long time since Raven felt really proud of something she had accomplished. It felt damn good, and she was going to savor it for as long as she could. In their line of work the everyday grind of saving lives went unnoticed by most which was fine, but Raven had been doing it for so long it was hard to get those early feelings of pride she once had when a job was done well. So yeah, she was going to soak up this experience for a minute.

CHAPTER 5

Suddenly the crowd began to clap, even the hunters who they had outwitted. The one who had tried to stop them at the end walked over and held out his hand to her. She looked at it then grasped it letting him pull her up.

"Congratulations." His tone was deep and serious just before a smile appeared on his face. He then reached down for Katrina who he also helped up. "I have to say I have never been more impressed. Which one of you is the animal whisperer?"

Katrina hobbled slightly, then steadied herself on her good leg. "That would be me."

He gave her a nod. "Some would call that cheating."

"How can you cheat when there are no rules." Katrina cocked her eyebrow at him. "And some would say calling someone a cheater is being a sore loser."

"Ouch." He said, then laughed before shaking Daniel's hand. "Good job, guys. And good takedown."

"Thanks." Daniel said with a nod.

Raven helped steady Katrina as the guy walked away. She saw Blaze and the rest of the Warriors trying to make their way through the crowd toward them. She glanced at Stanley. "Good job, Stan. We couldn't have done it without you."

"It's me that should be thanking you guys." Stanley said taking Katrina's other side as they made their way toward Blaze and the rest of them. The crowd of trainees and Warriors were thick. As they slowly made their way they were congratulated. "Maybe this will help me find a Mate."

Raven chuckled looking over at Stanley. "Dude this is going to definitely help you get laid." Raven laughed at the blush that brightened his face. "Listen, if you ever want to transfer to our team, I will definitely put in a good word for you."

"As will I." Daniel gave him a nod of respect.

Suddenly his team surrounded Stanley with pats on the back and Raven chuckled at the proud grin he wore on his face. "Think I'll be staying here. Thank you, Daniel, Raven, and Katrina. You ever need me just call." He said, then disappeared surrounded by the same trainees that didn't want him on their team.

"Are you okay?" Blaze finally made his way to Katrina picking her up.

"I'm fine." Katrina said, but her grimace said otherwise. "Just tweaked my leg when we jumped off that cliff."

"Yeah, about that." Blaze frowned at Raven. "Did you even know how deep that water was before you took my Mate over the edge?"

Raven frowned wondering how he knew they jumped into water. "Wait a minute. I looked for you among the other hunters at the first location and didn't see you. How did you know about that?"

"He had to bring in an injured trainee because Slade was busy with someone else. Everything was on camera." Sloan said as he walked up mid conversation. "Every hunter and observer had a go-pro attached to their vest for training purposes. We all watched it live."

"For the trainees or the hunters?" Raven said with a smirk. Yeah, she was feeling a little cocky.

Sloan actually laughed at that. "Well after what everyone just witnessed, I'd have to say both." He then looked at Katrina. "Your gift is priceless, Katrina. Good job out there."

"Thank you." Katrina said, then looked at Raven. "But honestly, it was Raven's plans that got us here. I just called in some friends to help."

"Well, I know my damn phone is going to be ringing off the hook with units wanting all three of you to transfer." Sloan's happy mood turned sour. "And I'm warning you now that if you even think of transferring, I will kill you all." With that said he turned and walked away.

"He gets a little uptight when he's happy." Jared said watching Sloan stomp away, then he pulled Raven in for a hug. "Good job. You do know that you guys are the only ones that made it. No one could figure out how to get past the hunters. They tried, but everyone failed but you guys."

"Failure was not an option." Raven said as she pulled away. She glanced around to see if Charger had come with Jared but didn't see him. She pushed the disappointment she felt deep where she kept all of her mixed feelings for Charger and smiled. "Guess I get that from you, huh?"

Something flashed across Jared's face before he returned her smile. "No, you actually get that from your mother." He placed a kiss on her forehead, then turned to congratulate Katrina who was still in Blaze's arms.

"Tracy would have been so proud of you today." Jake's voice had her spinning around. She looked up into his eyes that held a little life as he stared down at her. "As am I, Raven. You kicked some major ass out there."

She couldn't help it, she reached out and hugged him so tight she thought she might have knocked the wind out of him. "This one was for her, Jake." She whispered against his chest as she kept her tears from falling. She felt him shudder, but then was ripped from his arms.

"Don't hog her, Jake." Kane said as he slammed her into a hug. "Damn proud of you, Raven. Though you will always be a Dark Guardian in my heart."

"You don't have a heart you son of a bitch." Jake snorted surprising Raven. He sounded like the old Jake, and it hit her emotions hard.

Raven pulled away from Kane. "Thanks." She said, but her eyes were on Jake's back as he passed them.

"He's coming back." Kane whispered as he also watched Jake, then turned back toward her. "Slowly, but he's coming back. He won't ever be the same, but at least we are seeing more of him each day."

Raven nodded afraid of saying anything in fear of losing her shit and crying all over him. Kane gave her another quick hug then followed Jake. She watched them for a second before turning around. Charger stood there staring at her with a half-smile on his face. "What?"

"I knew you'd do it." Charger said with a proud tilt to his head as he looked at her.

"Oh, really." She cocked her eyebrow at him. "It didn't sound that way in the van earlier. Watch your ass, Raven. This is serious, Raven. You have enemies, Raven."

Charger frowned as he listened to her rant. "Yes, and all of that was true and had nothing to do with your abilities, *Raven*." He said adding a little attitude to her name.

"Whatever, Charger." Raven sighed tired of the back and forth with him. Some days she liked it, but not today. It seemed like they were always at odds, and it was getting old. She was mentally and physically exhausted as well as dirty. She needed a shower and a fucking hug from the asshole. Okay, where did that thought come from. Shaking her head, she went to pass him, but he stopped her.

"Why are you always…" He stopped seeming as if he was at a loss for words again. He seemed to always be at a loss of words with her.

"Always…what?" She questioned, but he remained silent just staring at her.

"Nothing." He said with a shake of his head.

Raven sighed. "Typical Charger answer." She turned to walk away from him, but he once again stopped her.

"Have you fed?" Charger asked, his voice low for just them to hear his words.

"Don't worry about it." Raven jerked her arm away from him. "I'm not your problem, nor will I ever be."

Free of his grip she walked toward where Slade was checking out Katrina. She knelt beside her. "How is it?" She asked trying to forget the conversation that went nowhere as usual with Charger.

"Sore." Katrina said with a smile. "But I'd do it again tomorrow."

"The fuck you will." Blaze, who knelt on the other side, growled. "Once is enough for me."

Raven rolled her eyes then looked at Slade. "Please tell me it's not broken."

"No, just sprained. She'll be fine once she feeds." Slade sat back with a frown. "You are both lucky. From the height you guys jumped hitting the water I'm sure it felt like hitting concrete."

"Pretty much sums it up." Raven winked at Katrina when Blaze growled again.

"Even vampires break, Raven." Slade said as he also stood up.

Raven didn't comment because she knew that very well. Thoughts of Tracy's broken body flashed through her mind, but she shook it off refusing to let the memories that haunted her every night when she was alone invade her thoughts while not alone.

"Hey!" Stanley rushed toward them. He glanced at Katrina and frowned. "You okay, Katrina?"

"Yeah, I'm good." Katrina said, then stood with the help of Blaze.

"I'm glad." Stanley said with a huge smile. The transformation from the first time they met him to now was amazing. He seemed more confident and happier. It was nice to see. "Listen, a bunch of us are getting together tonight at this place called Dawn Breakers down on the river before we all head out. Someone said it was a good vamp hangout. Will you guys come?"

"Can we go?" Katrina looked up at Blaze pleadingly.

"As long as your leg is better, yes, we can go." Blaze said, then laughed when she hugged him.

When Stanley looked at Raven hopefully, she smiled. "I'll be there." She laughed when he gave her a hug, then went to give one to Katrina, but stopped when Blaze glared down at him.

"Ah, great." He backed away quickly. "I'll see you guys later." She watched as he headed toward Daniel who was talking with Duncan.

"You're a bully." Raven shook her head at Blaze as they headed toward the vans.

"I am not." Blaze responded picking up Katrina so she didn't have to walk. "No one touches my Mate, but me."

"It was just a hug, Blaze." Katrina rolled her eyes, but Raven could see the love she had for Blaze.

It actually made Raven's heart hurt. What would it be like to have that with someone? Unfortunately, she had a feeling she would never know. It just didn't seem to be in the cards for her. Maybe she was just too…hell, she didn't even know the word that would describe her best. Too mannish maybe? Outspoken? Moody? Unlovable? That last descriptive word had her slowing slightly. It had just popped into her brain. Was she truly unlovable and if so, did she really care?

So deep in thought she stopped realizing they were at the van. Blaze was taking his car with Katrina but made sure she made it to the van. After telling them goodbye she stepped in the back and sat down. The word unlovable kept ringing in her ears and it frightened her.

Glancing up she saw that Kent along with the ones on his team heading toward Daniel who was walking her way. Kent shoved Daniel from behind. When he fell to the ground Raven took off.

"Fucking freak!" Kent growled as Daniel picked himself up and turned slowly toward him. "What in the hell is your problem? We lost because of you."

Daniel stopped Raven as she flew toward Kent. "No. You lost because you were more focused on taking Raven out than besting the Hunters."

Kent looked around nervously at the crowd that was surrounding them. "That's bullshit." Kent said, but his voice betrayed him. "You're a fucking liar."

With two strides Daniel was in Kent's face. "One thing you need to learn about me is that I never lie." Daniel growled; his odd eye color swirled making his eyes look cloudy. "And if you call me a liar one more time, I will make sure you regret those words. Do you understand me?"

"Fuck you and that bitch." Kent hissed leaning closer. Neither of them was touching the other, but with a quick nod of

Daniel's head Kent flew backwards hitting the ground hard.

Daniel was on him within seconds, his booted foot on Kent's chest. Kent tried to move but couldn't. It was as if he was being held down by not only Daniel's boot, but an unseen force. "You don't want to cross me, Kent." Daniel said, then looked up at his buddies. "None of you do. I suggest you take your loss and shut the fuck up. And if you ever think to do harm to Raven or any of the other trainees you will deal with me."

"Must be nice to have a daddy high up on the VC payroll." Kent sneered up at him and Raven wanted nothing more than to kick Kent's ass.

Daniel reached down grabbing Kent's shirt and picking him up to look him straight in the eyes. "My father has nothing to do with this nor will he ever. Which is a very bad thing for you because in all honesty he'd be the only one to save you from me. Hear my words, Kent. If you ever cross me or anyone close to me again, I promise you that nothing will save you. Not only do I not lie…I never break a promise."

"Here comes Sloan." Adam whispered the warning.

Raven glanced up to see Sloan frowning his way toward them. Duncan stood in the background watching but remained where he was as did Charger. She had mad respect for Duncan to allow Daniel to take care of his issue with Kent.

"What the fuck is going on?" Sloan asked just as Daniel let go of Kent smoothing down his shirt with a hard swipe.

"Nothing." Kent finally said after a long pause, but Daniel remained silent.

"Daniel?" Sloan said gaining his attention.

"It's been taken care of." Daniel replied, then turned to leave.

"I want to see you in my office as soon as we get back." Sloan ordered Daniel who continued to walk away.

"Yes, sir." Daniel replied respectfully.

Everyone watched as Daniel walked away as calm as if nothing had even happened. "Damn, that's bad ass." Steve whispered beside her. "It was as if it was yesterday, he was in diapers. Crazy shit."

Raven had to agree. Daniel was different in so many ways, but Steve was right. He had an air of bad ass surrounding him that seemed crazy, but it was there. Raven respected the hell out of the kid.

"Well, are we going to stand here all day with our dicks in our hands?" Sloan growled glaring at each of them. "Get in the fucking vans. Let's go!"

Raven rolled her eyes as she turned and headed toward the van. She didn't even have a response to that. Kent had totally killed her jovial mood which had now turned dark. Climbing into the back of the van she noticed that Kent and his buddies decided on the other van. Smart move on their part. It would take nothing for her to thrust kick their asses through the metal of the van into oncoming traffic. Hopefully Charger did the same thing. Yeah, she wasn't that lucky. Charger got in and closed the door. Her eyes met Charger's golden gaze before her own golden eyes slowly closed. The rocking of the moving van blocked everything out and she fell deeper into the dark mood she was most comfortable in…the place where the unlovable go.

CHAPTER 6

As the vans pulled up to the compound, Raven opened her eyes after hearing everyone file out. Even Charger was gone, and she was alone inside the van. With a sigh she climbed out herself and stretched. Planning on taking off, she frowned when she saw Daniel walking up the steps toward the compound behind Duncan, Charger, and Sloan. With a curse she headed that way. She wouldn't let him face this shit alone because she knew it was about what just happened with Kent which was really about her.

"Fuck." She cursed heading that way.

"I thought you'd be all smiles after what I heard happened today." Ryker's voice sounded behind her. "Congratulations."

"Thanks." Raven grinned at him as he fell in step beside her. "Where were you? I thought for sure you'd be there hunting someone."

"Sloan had me on other duties. The bad guys don't stop for Warrior initiation." Ryker said as he swiped his card and held the door open for her. "So did your 'fuck' mean this is a walk of doom or are you just hungry and heading for the kitchen realizing that Sid hasn't even started cooking yet?"

Raven laughed shaking her head. Ryker had a way of making her smile. "Doom I'm sorry to say."

"Well after you are finished and if you are still alive you need to give Susan a call." Ryker said stopping in front of Sloan's office. "She's been trying to call you all afternoon. Called me in a panic thinking something happened to you."

"Well did you tell her I had initiation?" Raven said, then realized how stupid that question was.

"We were sworn to secrecy to keep everyone safe." Ryker gave her a look indicating she should know this. "I told her you had a hot date last night and probably was still sowing your wild oats."

"You didn't." Raven glared at him horrified. "Please say you didn't."

"Oh, I did." Ryker chuckled with a hint of pure evilness. "Be prepared for a lot of questions."

"Paybacks a bitch, dude." Raven warned him then cocked her eyebrow. It would take her days and proof to get Susan to believe Ryker was full of shit and that she did have initiation, not a hot date. "So, you seem to be pretty chummy with my friend lately. Susan has your number, huh?"

A huge grin broke across Ryker's face. "Play with fire Raven and you will get burned."

"Right back at ya, bud." Raven gave him a look before turning and heading into Sloan's office without knocking hearing Ryker's laughter behind her.

"What do you want?" Sloan asked in his usual 'get the fuck out of my office' voice.

"Nothing." Raven said as she found a place on the wall and leaned against it.

"This doesn't concern you." Sloan's growled comment would intimidate most, and if she was being truthful at times Sloan made her want to turn around and walk quickly away from him. She would never admit that, but she wasn't a stupid person. Glancing at Daniel who was staring at her with a half grin she glanced back at Sloan.

"If this is about what happened with Kent then it definitely concerns me." Raven said, then added. "If not for Daniel my team's mission would have been compromised. And to be honest I don't know exactly what happened because at the time we were trying to save our asses and win so you and this unit didn't look like pussies. I'd say a thanks and a welcome mat in front of your door would be appropriate."

She noticed Jared swiped his hand across his face trying to hide his grin. Sid didn't even attempt to hide his, he just plain out grinned with a chuckle. As for Charger he just glared at her...shocker. And Duncan was as serious as always, no emotion whatsoever on his handsome face. Sloan however looked as if he wanted to choke the life out of her and bury her in the welcome mat she just mentioned. Maybe she needed to curb her attitude just a little bit.

"Raven please don't make me regret taking you on by acting like Jared." Sloan's voice sounded calm which kind of scared her. "I've never killed a woman in my life, and I don't want to start now. Keep your fucking smart-ass comments to yourself before you are my first."

"I will do my best..." Raven said with a nod, then added, "sir."

"Nice touch." Sid said with an appreciative nod.

"Shut the fuck up, Sid." Sloan ordered then looked at Daniel. "What happened between you and Kent?"

"I told you, it's taken care of." Daniel said, then frowned. "I don't mean any disrespect, but I don't want them kicked out. It's between him and me now."

"And me." Raven said with a cocked eyebrow.

"Yeah, not so much." Daniel glanced at her. "I've pretty much taken the heat off you which was the plan."

"I didn't expect you to do that." Raven frowned not liking being indebted to anyone.

"You knocked them out, Daniel." Duncan said with a frown. "And we want to know exactly why. When the Hunters chased you, we saw them lined against the tree. The only one standing was Kent."

"That's because I smacked the shit out of him to wake him." Raven said with a shrug when everyone including Daniel stared at her with wide eyes. "Hey, I didn't want the blame for them losing and I knew I would definitely get the blame. So, I gave him a smack to wake his ass up"

"Daniel, I need to know what kind of men..." Sloan said, then glanced at Raven. "and women I have joining my ranks. If they are not trustworthy, I cannot put others in my charge in danger."

"He's an asshole who has something against Raven or just women in general." Daniel shrugged, then gave Raven an apologetic glance. "Unfortunately, he isn't going to be the only one. You run every guy out that has a problem with women in a man's world, then you are going to be shorthanded."

Sloan was silent for a long minute. "Well for saying a lot that didn't tell me shit. Or at least shit I didn't already know." Sloan ran his hand down his face. "You're free to go." He told Daniel with a nod.

"You'll have to ask him why he and his team were sneaking up behind Raven. Maybe I'm wrong, but it didn't sit well with me, so I did what I had to do for my team. Don't get rid of him on my account." Daniel said as he walked toward the door. "I'm sure I have a lot of assholes in my future so I'm using him as practice."

Raven grinned at that. Daniel really didn't give two shits about Kent and neither did she. "Not on my account either." Raven added following Daniel out of Sloan's office. Reaching out she stopped Daniel. "Thanks Daniel. I appreciate you having my back. I owe you one."

Daniel smiled, his eyes swirling as he stared at her. "I know you do." He finally said, then his smile slipped. "You need to feed soon, Raven. If Charger won't do it, then find someone who will but it needs to be soon."

In Daniel fashion he turned and headed toward the kitchen without saying another word. With a shake of her head, she started toward the door just as Charger came out of Sloan's office. Daniel was right she needed to feed. She felt the dark hunger rising inside her which was never a good thing for a vampire. Raven knew she was pushing it by not feeding regular like all Warriors as well as Dark Guardians were expected to do.

What no one understood other than female vampires is that it was harder for women to find blood donors. Most male donors expected sex in return and well that wasn't going to happen with Raven. It got to the point she just didn't want to deal with it, which in turn, had her on edge when it was time for her to feed.

"What?" Charger's voice broke through her thoughts.

She almost…almost asked him to let her feed from him, but her brain stopped her mouth before the words slipped out. "What?" She said in return.

"You're standing there looking at me." Charger replied as an arrogant smirk formed on his lips. "I figured you wanted something from…me."

"Don't flatter yourself." Raven snorted, but in truth it was exactly about him…the asshole.

"Hey Raven." Daniel called out from behind them. She turned to see him walking toward them with a plate piled high with food. "If you're having trouble finding a donor talk to Jill. She had the same issue."

Raven could see Charger's face change from smirky to angry from her peripheral vision. Fuck, that was the last damn thing she wanted him to know. "I'm not having issues, Daniel, but thanks. Got it set up already." She totally lied, hopefully successfully. Not waiting around to see she turned and headed toward the door. "Later." Raven said just as she closed the door behind her.

Once outside she hurried toward where her bike was usually parked, but remembered it was at the damn warehouse. Cursing she took off at a run. It wasn't far and honestly, she needed to clear her mind and a run might just do the trick. "Yeah, right, like that is going to clear all the shit in my head." She said to herself as she took off.

She was right, it didn't. If anything, it made it worse and by the time she got to her bike she pulled her phone out and sent off a text. Within seconds she received a reply. Glancing at the time she climbed on her bike, put her phone back in her pocket and then took off. She had just enough time to shower before her blood donor showed up. Daniel was right and she just needed to bite the bullet and fucking feed.

Raven had texted Lee, who she had used twice before. He was polite and didn't get weird, but the last time she had fed from him Lee had asked her to dinner. That was the last time she used him, and it sucked. Even when her and Charger was doing okay, it was always in the back of her mind that if she couldn't feed from Charger, she would be back at square one. Story of her freaking life.

Pulling into her place she got off her bike, stretched then headed inside. The place was starting to get that homey feeling, or at least what she thought was homey. She was getting comfortable there, spending time with herself which was new to her. Usually when she spent too much alone time her demons came knocking in her memories and she didn't have time for a breakdown.

Grabbing some clean clothes she rushed to the bathroom, flipped on the water, undressed, and took the quickest shower she had ever taken. Hearing her phone ringing she cursed as she dressed which was made harder by not drying completely off. Grabbing her phone, she answered it before actually looking to see who was calling.

"Better be important." She answered harshly.

"Someone needs to teach you phone etiquette." Susan's voice came over the line making Raven smile.

Raven rolled her eyes heading toward her bedroom to finish getting dressed. "You want me nice, then text me. You know I hate talking on the phone."

"This isn't a text kind of call." Susan snorted. "I thought we were friends, Raven."

"Um, we are when you're not pissing me off." Raven said with a smirk even though Susan couldn't see her, but Susan knew her well and she waited for it.

"Wipe that smirk off your face." Susan didn't disappoint. "Who doesn't piss you off? Wasn't it you last week who got pissy with that older lady?"

"I was in a hurry." Raven frowned remembering it well because Susan tore into her ass.

"She was on a cane, Raven." Susan sighed with a hiss.

Raven grimaced as she finished with her boots. Susan was right and Raven had felt bad for being so impatient. She loved old people, just not when she was in a hurry. "What do you want Susan? I've got a few things to do before I head over, can this wait?"

"No, it cannot fucking wait." Susan said dramatically. "Didn't you see your missed calls and texts from me? Good damn thing I wasn't laying in a ditch and dying somewhere needing help from my…*friend*."

Raven had Susan on speaker phone. After finishing putting on her boots, she reached for it and checked her missed calls. Damn, that was a lot of missed calls. "You sound pretty healthy to me." Raven replied, yet she knew she needed to get better with checking her messages, but dammit she hated the phone and missed the days when they didn't have them. Life was easier back then.

"Wow." Susan said, laying it on thick with her fake hurt voice. "Just wow."

"I'm sorry. I'm glad you're okay. Is that better?" Raven walked into her kitchen and opened the fridge. It was completely empty. "Now what was so important you left fifty messages on my phone that I now have to delete."

"You're a dick." Susan said making Raven grin as she shut the fridge door then leaned against it.

"I know." Raven's smile grew. She would die for Susan. With no hesitation whatsoever. They gave each other shit, but she would lay down her life for the human just as she would have for Tracy. "Unless you want to leave more messages you best tell me what's up."

"I'm very upset that I had to find out from Ryker that my best friend had a hot date that lasted into the next day." Susan's tone rose with each word. "That's what's up."

"Ryker seems to be hanging around a lot lately." Raven grinned knowing how to get under Susan's skin.

"Don't you dare turn this around on me." Susan warned sternly over the phone. "I want to know who this guy is, how did you meet him, his name, color hair, height, is he vampire or human, and was his wang big enough to make you scream?"

"His wang?" The names Susan came up with for guys cocks always cracked her up. "You mean his penis?"

"Ugh, I hate that word." Susan made a gagging sound. "And yes, did he have a nice wang?"

"Well, I don't know Susan." Raven replied just as someone knocked on her front door. "You'll have to ask Ryker how big his…wang is since he made the guy up. Listen I have to go I'll talk to you later."

"Made him up? What?" Susan said confused. "Don't you dare hang…"

Raven did hang up just as she opened the door. "Hey Lee." Raven smiled at the handsome vampire. "Come on in."

CHAPTER 7

Charger stared at the door Raven just walked out of trying to control his rage. Who the fuck is she feeding from? Did he know him? Why did that even matter? Charger frowned knowing exactly why that mattered. He would hate to kill someone he knew.

"You just going to stand there staring at the door or are you going to go after her?" Daniel's voice broke him from his chaotic thoughts.

"It's none of my business who she feeds from." He said realizing he growled those words with so much anger his jaw felt locked from clenching his teeth.

Daniel forked some food in his mouth with a grin and chewed as he stared at Charger. "Yeah, okay." Daniel chuckled knowingly which pissed Charger off even more. Daniel moved past Charger and with his plate of food headed toward the stairs leading up to the living quarters of the compound.

Charger cursed under his breath. "Who is she feeding from?" Damn he hated asking that question.

Stopping Daniel turned halfway up the steps then sat down. "Even if I knew I wouldn't tell you Charger. Either let her go or claim her. It's an easy decision."

"Kid, all you know is easy." Charger frowned at Daniel. "Nothing about that statement is easy."

"You can be a dick to me all you want because honestly I don't care." Daniel shoved more food in his mouth as if what he said was true. He didn't give a shit. "But when I see someone intentionally hurting someone when that doesn't have to happen then I'll have my say. You don't have to like it. You don't have to like me. But you will lose her and when you do, I will be first in line to tell you I told you so dumbass."

Charger was silent for a few minutes absorbing what Daniel said. "You know I'm not afraid of your father." He finally broke the silence. "I will kick your ass if need be."

"I don't need my father to fight my battles anymore. And give me a few months and I won't be that easily beaten." Daniel stood then turned heading up the steps. "And Charger." He said without stopping.

"Yeah?" Charger called up as Daniel neared the top.

"Nothing about my life has been or will be easy." Daniel had stopped at the top of the steps then looked back at Charger over his shoulder. "Don't mistake the age I was to who I am now. That will be a mistake many will make. Don't be one of the many."

Charger stared at the empty staircase then shook his head. "What the fuck?"

"The kid has a way about him." Kane said from behind Charger.

"Yeah." Charger replied, then turned toward Kane. "You going to feed Raven?"

"Fuck no." Kane snorted with a narrowed look toward Charger. "I want to live."

"Shit." Charger cursed cracking his neck from side to side.

"Wait a minute." Kane frowned, all teasing aside. "You haven't been feeding her?"

Charger shook his head. "Not since Tracy and the whole Jake thing."

"What the fuck, man." Kane's tone turned angry. "I know she isn't part of the Guardians, but still. If I would have known I would have made sure she was taken care of, but dammit Charger I don't give a fuck what you say, that is your job."

Kane was right. It was his fucking job because he was her maker. He had changed her. Even if there wasn't anything between them on a personal basis, his being her maker trumped all of it. If she was in need, in danger or anything it was his responsibility to make sure she was taken care of no matter what he said in the past.

"Listen I will take care of her because you know you can trust me not to make any moves. As much as I fuck around and say shit, Raven is like a sister to me." Kane clapped him on the back. "But I'm telling you right now no other man is going to make that promise to you."

"Thanks, Kane." Charger gave him a nod then spotted Adam heading toward them. "Hey, I need you to tell me where Raven is."

"Ah, man." Adam frowned shaking his head. "Raven scares the shit out of me. She warned me never to pry into her mind."

"I totally heard her warning." Steve walked up next to Adam with a serious look on his face. "I say walk away buddy. Not worth it."

Kane actually laughed shaking his head. "So, you are more afraid of Raven than you are of Charger and for shits and giggles I'll add myself."

"Damn, now that's a pickle." Steve rubbed his chin looking between Kane and Charger. "Nah, I'm still going with Raven."

Both Kane and Charger glared at Steve. "Seriously?" Kane wasn't laughing now. "Do you even know what I could do to you?"

"Ah, thought we were talking about Adam." Steve didn't look too sure now, but then he shrugged. "Have you ever had a woman pissed off at you? I mean seriously pissed one off. Well, I have."

"Shocker." Kane mumbled and Charger agreed. Steve pissed a lot of people off and on a daily basis.

"They can be fucking mean and very, ah, creative in their paybacks. I mean ruthless. You don't even know it's coming, man." Steve continued his eyes widened as if he remembered such a time, but then he focused again. "With Raven you add those with her kickass skills, then yeah, I would take my chances with you two before I would Raven. That is if we were talking about me, but we aren't. Adam's ass is on the line, not mine."

"He has a point." Kane said after a moment of thought.

"She's at her place." Adam said ignoring Steve's advice.

"Your funeral." Steve whispered to Adam shaking his head as if his friend was already six feet deep.

"Thanks." Charger gave him a nod then turned toward the door.

"But you may want to call ahead." Adam added the warning. "Looks like she has company."

"Told ya so." Kane cocked his eyebrow at Charger. "You're fucking up, brother. Dumbass."

"Fuck you, Kane." Slamming out of the compound Charger headed for his bike. His body vibrated with anger as well as the need to get to Raven before she took another man's blood. Kane was right he was a dumbass. He should have taken control when he knew she had to feed, but instead he stepped back like he always fucking did when it came to Raven.

Climbing on his bike he grabbed his phone and stared at it. What was he going to do? Call her and tell her not to feed? Knowing Raven as well as he did, she would do it just to fucking do what he said not to do. Putting his phone back into his pocket he took off. It was time he and Raven had a long talk.

∼

Raven stood in her kitchen with Lee having small talk. She had never been comfortable with feeding from donors. With the uptick of female Warriors and Guardians male donors were becoming more common, which was a good thing and yet, Raven hated it. Having to depend on full blood vampires to survive sucked.

"So, I hear you've transferred from the Guardians to the VC." Lee said taking her out of her thoughts.

"I'm sure you have." Raven snorted offering Lee a beer. He took it with a nod of thanks. "As I'm sure you've heard that I'm a traitor to the Guardians."

Lee grinned taking a drink from the bottle before setting it down on the counter. "That word may have been mentioned a time or two."

Raven rolled her eyes taking her own drink of beer. Even though it took a ton of alcohol for a vampire to get drunk she liked the taste and a few beers seemed to relax her somewhat. "Yeah, figured that."

"Hey, who cares what anyone else thinks." Lee said with a shrug. "If that was the move you had to make then what does it matter what others think."

"The Guardians are a pretty tight group." Raven said as if that explained it.

"So are the Warriors from what I hear." Lee countered. "Would the Guardians except a Warrior transfer?"

Thinking of her father, Jared, she nodded. "For the most part yes, they would."

As they stood there casually talking Raven realized after her second beer, she wasn't feeling relaxed at all. If anything, she was more anxious. She also noticed Lee was being more brazen than the other few times letting his eyes roam her body.

Their small talk dwindled to silence, and she had a bad feeling he was expecting more than a thank you for his services. Donors got paid by the VC, but there were times they got a nice tip and she wasn't talking money. Taking of blood was sexual for most vampires. It took control to keep from acting on those urges. Her control was extreme unless it was Charger. Fucking Charger. Always Charger. She had no control when it came to that man, and she knew it. What was worse he knew it also.

So many times she had wanted to just say, fuck it, and let herself go into someone else's arms. She had once, only once and it had been the worst time of her life. She had been miserable and made others miserable. Her thoughts went to Val as guilt swirled inside her.

"So, are you ready to do this?" Lee said breaking into her thoughts.

"Hmmm?" She focused on him then cleared her throat. "Oh, yeah. Let me throw these away first."

Raven cursed silently at herself as she turned to toss the empty beer bottles in the trash. Dammit, she was losing her mind because all she wanted to do was turn back around and send Lee on his way. She didn't want his blood. Not a single drop and yet her stomach clinched in agony from hunger. She knew she was on the edge of blood lust; she could feel it creeping in the shadows she kept hidden from everyone.

She also knew he was expecting something from her in return and she didn't want to deal with that. It was also messy, ended up her having to kick someone's ass and well, she was just tired. Mentally tired. Fucking Charger. This was all his fault and if he was here right now she would tell him exactly that... the fucker.

A loud pounding on her door had her turning around. The first thing she saw was Lee standing behind her with his shirt off. "What are you doing?" Raven ignored the pounding on her door as she glared up at Lee.

"I don't want to get blood on my shirt." He replied looking innocent, but she knew he wasn't innocent at all. The two times she had fed from him before had been from the wrist. That had been and was still her rule. Safer that way. Less touching, etc.

Glancing at the door she frowned first at it, then back up at Lee. "Not happening, Lee." She informed him with a cocked eyebrow. "Wrist or not at all. Put your shirt back on."

She walked around him with a warning glare not to touch her as she headed toward the door where the pounding was getting louder to the point it was rattling dangerously on the hinges. "Hold on, dammit!" She shouted.

"They were right. You are a tease." Lee said from behind her stopping her cold in her tracks. Turning she glared at him.

"What did you just say?" Raven growled her eyes glowing black.

Lee went to grab the shirt he had tossed on a chair just as the door burst opened. Raven turned in defense mode ready to take out whoever just broke her fucking door only to see Charger staring at her before his rage filled eyes fell on Lee.

For some strange reason Raven quickly glanced around her newly furnished place and had a feeling it was all going to go to shit. She had put a lot of hard work into her home to make it her own and well, yeah, she had a feeling it was about to be demolished and by the look on Charger's face seeing a shirtless Lee she was right.

CHAPTER 8

Charger's eyes narrowed as he stormed toward Lee. Raven had seen Charger angry before, but something in his eyes told her this was different. This wasn't good. Not good at all.

"Charger." Raven warned stepping in front of him, but Charger just picked her up and placed her to the side as if she was nothing but a slip of paper. "Dammit, I just furnished this place."

Ignoring her Charger grabbed the shirt slamming it into the man's chest causing him to stumble backwards. "Get the fuck out."

"Who the fuck are you?" The man steadied himself glaring at Charger.

"The man who is seconds away from fucking up your world." Charger leaned toward him with a growl. "Permanently."

Okay, as bad as this was Raven had to admit that Charger was fucking hot when he was angry. Right now, he was raging, and she felt her body come alive with so much sexual tension she was about to snap. What in the hell was wrong with her? Was she losing her damn mind? She should be pissed that Charger stormed into her domain as if he owned the place, owned her. She should be livid, not turned on to the point she wanted to throw Lee out herself and fuck Charger senseless. Seriously, was she that hard up for sex? Knowing the answer to that, which was a big fat fucking yes, she frowned pissed more at herself than anyone else.

"He's a blood donor, Charger." Raven said, her voice shaking with anger. "You have no right to come here, breaking down my door and being rude to my guest." She kept the part of him turning her on to herself because he definitely had no right to do that or know that…the asshole.

"Your shirtless guest has a fucking hard-on." Charger's voice turned deadly as he glared at her. "Donating blood isn't the only fucking thing on his mind."

Raven's eyes, of course, went to Lee's bulge and nothing happened. She felt nothing. She didn't even wonder how big he was which was kind of amazing. Hey, she couldn't help her thought process and she always wondered. Most women did and if they said they didn't they were liars.

Her eyes rose as she shook her head. "Blood was the only agreement we had, Lee. Nothing more."

"Maybe if you hadn't been such a tease, you'd find out what you've been missing." Lee gave her a cocky grin that Charger quickly punched right off his face. And that is when shit went down in her newly furnished living room. Honestly if Charger hadn't punched him first, she would have. What an arrogant dick.

Raven cringed as Lee tried to tackle Charger sending them heading toward the new lamp that had just been delivered two days ago. With a quick dive she grabbed the lamp just as the men hit the floor crashing into her coffee table. "Shit." Raven put the lamp in, hopefully, a safe corner then headed toward the men. Charger was on top of Lee raining down blow after blow. It really wasn't a fair fight at all. Lee was getting his ass kicked. "Stop!" Raven ordered, but Charger was obviously past hearing anything she had to say.

Lee managed to slip in a punch that snapped Charger's head back, but only seemed to piss him off more. "Get up!" Charger demanded as he stood then backed away slightly. "Come on, asshole. Maybe next time you'll think twice before talking to a lady with disrespect."

Lady? Okay, that was a first. Charger had never called *her* a lady and she probably would have cursed him out if he had. Rolling her eyes Raven went to stand between them, but Lee jumped to his feet swinging, missing and then Charger started landing blows again. This totally wasn't a fair fight. Lee stumbled back and Raven watched in horror as he was heading straight toward the small antique table she had found at a yard sale on her way home one day. Dammit, she really liked that table. It looks like it had seen a lot, just like her and she felt connected to it.

Rushing that way, she pushed Lee to the side so she could block her small table. She was about to order them to take it outside but stopped. She hadn't lived here very long and didn't think having two men fighting outside her place was the neighborly thing to do. Lee's head snapped back from another punch to the mouth almost knocking a picture of sunflowers off the wall. Dammit!

"Enough!" Raven yelled loud enough that both men stopped to look at her. She pointed at Charger. "You stop it and you…get out." She ordered Lee.

Lee swiped at the blood pouring out of his nose. "You will never have another donor knocking on your door."

"Yeah, well, whatever." Raven shrugged. What was new. Shit that hit the fan always seemed to splatter on her anyway. She was used to it and yet, she'd find a way to feed herself. "Just get out."

Charger bent grabbing Lee's shirt throwing it at him, then growled when Lee continued to stand there as if he wanted to say more. "One more word and they will carry you out of here in a body bag."

Raven watched as Lee walked out the door then went to close it, but it was off the hinges so she couldn't even have the satisfaction of slamming it. "Shit!"

"I'll fix the fucking door, Raven." Charger said in a tone she didn't appreciate. He headed toward the door stepping over her broken table. "And buy you a new table."

When he passed her, she smelled blood and she knew his smell, it was Charger's blood. There wasn't much because Lee only landed one good punch. Her stomach tightened in hunger and her desire shot up past any level she thought she had. She took in a deep breath as he passed. He must have heard because he stopped, his body tightened and yet, he didn't turn around. Within a second, he was walking toward the door, studied it, and then lifted it putting it back on the hinge.

Raven's eyes roamed the muscles through his tight shirt as he worked to fix her door. He hadn't hit it hard enough to totally break it, but enough that it was taking him a minute to get it to close and lock right. Pulling her eyes off him she walked over and picked up her lamp putting it back on the table. She then bent and started to clean up her busted table. A pair of boots caught her vision as she looked slowly up to see Charger standing over her, his eyes burning into hers.

"I'm sorry about your table." He said but didn't really sound sorry at all. That was Charger. If an ass had to be beaten, he would do it without apology and then fix or buy whatever was broken in the process.

"What are you doing here, Charger?" Raven stood holding the broken piece of her table and realized she could just as easily be holding the broken pieces of her heart. A heart he had torn into shreds multiple times and yet, here she was yearning for him. Jesus, she needed to get her head out of her ass where he was concerned.

"You need to feed." Charger replied the obvious.

"I said I had it taken care of." Raven replied trying not to stare too deeply into those golden eyes framed with long black lashes. "And I did until you burst through my door."

His eyes darkened dangerously. "Feeding you was not the only thing he wanted to do."

"Charger, I'm not a slut. Feeding was all that was going to happen, or I would have happily kicked his ass out. And I would have done it without breaking my stuff." Raven huffed as she turned away from him to dump the broken pieces she held into the trash, but he stopped her turning her back around to face him.

"I never said you were a slut." Charger growled down at her, his lips deepened into a scowl.

Raven ignored that as she pulled away from him which he let her do and walked to the trash. She stood facing away from him even after her arms were empty. "Charger, I know you feel responsible for me because it was you who turned me. I get it, but honestly, I just can't take this anymore." She finally turned around to face him.

"What do you mean? Can't take what anymore?" Charger's scowl deepened even further if that was possible, and his eyes narrowed.

"Us. You and me, this back and forth." Raven pointed at him then herself before doing it quickly as if trying to prove a point. "Aren't you tired? I know I am. I never know what I'm going to get with you. One minute you hate me, the next minute I'm a pain in your ass and then the next we are…"

Charger took a step closer, but didn't reach out to touch her. "We are…what?"

"Fucking like there is no tomorrow. Like nothing matters except us." Raven frowned hating to be pouring out her feelings like this, but for the first time in a long time she was being totally honest with him. "I can't keep doing this. I haven't fed since the last time I fed from you, Charger. And it's not because I don't need it. I'm on the edge. I feel that dark hunger bubbling up inside me right now just waiting for me to crack so the blood lust can begin."

"Raven—" Charger started, but she stopped him.

"No, let me finish. I have to have my say now that I've started." Raven waved him away. "There are not many male blood donors. Lee is the only one that never expected anything from me, well at least until tonight. I refuse to ask any of the Warriors because of the respect I have for their Mates, and I refuse to ask any of the Guardians. And honestly, as dumb as this sounds, to feed from anyone but you makes me feel like I'm cheating on you."

Raven said, then laughed shaking her head and she couldn't stop laughing. It was crazy. Sounded crazy. She was fucking crazy and the exact reason for that was standing there staring at her like she was crazy.

"I'm losing my mind." She said between laughter, then a tear fell from one eye and rolled down her cheek. She angrily swiped it away leaving a smear of red across her cheek. "That is why I can't keep doing this Charger. And that is why you must walk away from me because I can't keep being your responsibility. It's slowly killing me. This needs to be over now, this minute or…"

She never got to finish because Charger was taking her in his arms. He held her so tight she felt crushed and yet she welcomed it for only a minute, but she started to pull away.

"I am your maker, Raven." He whispered into her hair not allowing her to pull away. "You will always be my responsibility."

"Then you will be my downfall." Raven whispered against his chest and knew she had hit her mark. His body went tense and stiff. All she could do now was push him so far away that he wouldn't want to have anything to do with her. She was done. This was it. She had said her piece and if all he saw her as was the human he had turned, then this ended now. It should have ended decades ago, but today she was finished. "Lock up when you leave."

With one final push he allowed her to walk away from him and into her bedroom where she closed the door. She bit her lip hard keeping her tears in check. She listened hoping and yet dreading to hear the front door close. For so long she had loved that man, would have gone through hellfire for him and this very moment she had ended it.

Her stomach churned with waves of hunger, sadness, and God she didn't know what else. Her chest heaved as she held in her sobs of absolute pain. Squeezing her eyes shut she tried to block out the look on his face as she was opening herself wide for him. There had been no emotion on his face other than that scowl that even made him as handsome as sin. She should hate him, but she didn't. Dammit she couldn't hate him.

Her door opened behind her and her whole body stiffened. "Please Charger. I can't."

She felt him come closer, it was as if their bodies close together were electrically charged. When his hands clasped her arms, she shuddered at the feeling of longing filling her soul. Slowly he turned her, but she kept her eyes tightly closed.

"Open them, Raven." Charger ordered; his voice had a certain command to it.

Slowly she opened them, his scowl was gone, but what replaced it was even worse. Her eyes searched his and what she saw reflected back at her was the same lost look she felt.

"If you go down…" He tipped her face up closer, his lips brushing close to hers. "so do I."

CHAPTER 9

Charger despised himself for putting Raven through the hell he had put her through. Repeatedly he told himself it was for her own good. He wasn't good enough for her. No man would ever be good enough for her. Many times she had told him that she wasn't his responsibility, but tonight was the first time she had actually told him to his face that he would be her downfall. He had heard those words loud and clear. Yet, he knew that letting her go was not something he could easily do, if ever.

Not much scared Charger, but losing Raven terrified him. When she had shut the door behind her after walking away from him Charger knew without a doubt that if he left now Raven would be lost to him forever.

Without hesitation he had walked to her bedroom door and opened it. He now stood in front of her not knowing what else to say. Her eyes stared up at him expectantly and Charger knew that this woman deserved so much more than what he had given her.

"Raven you are mine. You will always be mine." Charger started to speak but faltered when he saw the disappointment shining from her eyes. "But not because I was the one that changed you."

Shifting her eyes away from his Raven just shook her head.

Before she could speak, he continued. "I know I have said those words before, but dammit Raven I am a complicated man. And you are definitely a complicated woman." Her eyes shot back toward his and narrowed slightly, but then softened when she shrugged her agreement to that statement. "So, our relationship is going to be complicated. I'm not good at this shit, but you have to know what you mean to me."

"But I don't Charger and that's the problem." Raven whispered then cleared her throat. "I've never known your real feelings for me. I know you care just like you care about Kane. It's no different."

Okay, that surprised him. "Ah, yeah. My feelings for you are far different from Kane." Charger snorted. "How can you even think that, Raven?"

"The only difference I see is you don't tell him what he can and cannot do. You don't treat him like he has the plague when you don't want to be bothered with your feelings." Raven began listing things and Charger could feel himself getting aggravated but did his best to keep calm.

"I definitely don't want to fuck Kane." Charger added then cursed when her face fell, then turned angry.

"But you sure fucked plenty of women in front of me." Raven's eyes narrowed with attitude that he usually admired when it wasn't directed toward him. "So how does that make me feel special?"

"Oh, we are going to bring up the past now?" Charger felt his own attitude changing. "So, I guess we can talk about Val?"

"Do you really want to go there?" Raven cocked her eyebrow at him as she crossed her arms.

"Do you?" Charger cocked his own brow then crossed his arms in a mirrored image of her.

"What did you expect me to do? Keep my legs closed until you made a move. You kicked me out of your fucking bed, Charger. And I was sick and tired of watching you march women in and out of your bed so fuck you." Raven's voice rose as her eyes turned black as night. Damn she was beautiful when she was pissed off. Actually, she was the most beautiful woman he had ever seen, but when she was angry, she was radiant.

"So, you jumped in bed with a fellow Guardian?" Charger shot back. "I never touched another woman after Val left and you stopped fucking him. Fuck you right back."

He knew he had pushed her too far. Her breast was heaving with anger and his eyes fell to watch their rise and fall. Damn she had a nice set of tits on her and that's why he never saw the slap coming. It was so hard his head snapped back. Charger's eyes turned instantly black as he slowly looked at her. Before she could slap him again, he caught her wrist, used his body to push her against the wall.

Charger sneered down at her. "What in the hell was that for?"

"It felt good." She sneered right back as she tried to use her other hand to smack him a second time, but once again he stopped her. Now he had both her hands trapped in his.

"As I said...complicated." He smirked as he leaned closer to her, their lips almost touching. He watched as her tongue snaked out wetting her lips. He groaned low in his throat and felt his cock tighten. He put her trapped hands above her head against the wall. "Now what are you going to do, Raven?"

To his surprise her leg lifted running up his thigh then slowly toward his hardening cock. She tilted her head, her eyes watching his closely as she once again licked those full lips. Jesus, he had never seen anything as sexy as her licking those lips while he had her totally under his control. Just as that thought cleared his mind, he felt her give him a push and he was falling backwards. While he was watching her tongue play, she dropped her leg and trapped his foot successfully tripping him. Yeah, well two could play at that game. As they fell, he let go of her hands, wrapped one arm around her waist and turned them using his free hand to break their fall. She was now underneath him just where he wanted her to be.

"Good try." He gave her a cocky grin as he stared down into her eyes.

With a speed that should have made him proud she trapped the arm that was posted on the floor keeping all his weight off her while the other one was trapped underneath her waist. She quickly flipped him to where she was on top of him straddled across his hard cock. This time he heard her soft moan when she felt him through her jeans. She was leaned over to keep her base strong so he couldn't flip her, but in truth if he wanted her on her back again, she would be on her back, but the view here was too good to fuck with. Her shirt gaped open showing her full tits falling out of her bra as they pressed together. Soon he would have them in his mouth.

"Now what are you going to do, Charger?" She threw his words back at him.

"Many things." His gaze rose to hers and he didn't hide his desire. "That we are both going to enjoy."

~

Oh, shit, this wasn't supposed to happen Raven thought. She had to stand her ground, but damn feeling his hardness against her was making her brain turn traitor and her body turn slut. She wanted him and wanted him bad, but she made a promise to herself no more sex until he committed to something. She didn't really know what, but something. Dammit.

Feeling a little panicked she looked for an escape so she could get her bearings. If she let this happen things were never going to change. Scrambling she made her way off him, almost got to her feet but was tackled from behind.

"Dammit, Charger." Raven said but couldn't help the grin that slipped across her lips. He wanted a fight; she'd damn well give him one. Throwing her elbow back she felt it make contact with his stomach. His grip on her legs loosened and she half crawled toward the door until she made it to her feet, but she wasn't fast enough. Charger was on her, his front pressed against her back as he pushed her into the wall.

"Where you going?" Charger asked against her ear. "We aren't finished."

Raven tried to wiggle her way out of his grasp, but he moaned as her ass pressed against his hardness then moved away. Sighing whether in relief or disappointment she didn't know. She turned to say something but seeing him taking off his shirt all ability to form words left her. Her eyes roamed his broad shoulders, muscled chest that tapered into a tight six pack and narrowed into the waist band of his jeans. Before her eyes could go any lower they shot back up to his. The half grin he wore was like a splash of cold water.

"Not happening." Raven's voice cracked with need. She cleared her throat as she shook her head back and forth slowly. "I'm not having sex with you Charger." Damn that was hard to say because in all honesty her body was vibrating with need.

"I know."

"I mean it. I'm not having…" Raven frowned. "What did you say?"

"I said I know." Charger's grin grew. "Raven, I have never had to force a woman to have sex with me and I'm not starting now."

"Obviously since they couldn't stay out of your bed." Raven rolled her eyes with another snort. "What's your game?"

"No game." Charger replied without hesitation.

"Then why is your shirt off?" Her eyes narrowed knowing he was up to something.

"Before you walk out that door you are going to feed." Charger said innocently and she wasn't buying it.

"But you said that you were going to do many things we are both going to enjoy." Raven threw his own words at him.

"Yes." Charger nodded. "I did. And when you take my blood, I enjoy feeding you and I know you enjoy taking my blood."

"Oh." She frowned wrinkling her nose. "Well, ah, I'll take it from your wrist. So, you can put your shirt back on."

"Okay." Charger said picking up his shirt and putting it back on. "Do you want me to get it started."

Raven nodded still not trusting his motives. Something wasn't right. Charger never backed down and right now that's exactly what he was doing. Backing down. It was the unfortunate truth that if he wanted her on her back, she would be on her back naked for him. Yes, she was that weak when it came to this man and sometimes, she hated herself for that weakness.

She watched as he brought his wrist to his mouth and bit into his skin. The richness of his blood hit her senses and her fangs lengthened, her mouth watered, and her pussy clenched. Holy shit this was going to take a lot of control on her part.

Cautiously she took a few steps where Charger stood, his precious blood seeping from the wound he created for her. Slowly she took his wrist and brought it to her mouth. As soon as her lips touched his skin and the warm spicy blood hit her tongue she was lost. Raven took long hard pulls trying to get as much of his blood as she could. After what only seemed like seconds, which she knew it was much longer, she started to pull away. Charger stopped her.

"Take as much as you need, Raven." His voice was soothing, caring and she felt it straight to her soul. Damn him. "It's been a long time since you fed."

After a few more long tugs from his wrist, she reluctantly let it go. Slowly she licked his wound closed then wiped her mouth.

"Thank you." She finally said feeling shy, which was such a crazy emotion because she didn't have a shy bone in her body.

"You're welcome." He tipped her face up to his. "And Raven. I'm sorry for how I've treated you in the past, but that was the past. I hope from here on out we can leave it there."

"And does that go both ways?" Raven asked hoping that it did.

"Yes, it does." Charger replied with a nod. "I know it's going to be hard for you to believe me when I say I listened to you and I'm going to do everything in my power to make you realize it. But until then it will have to be you who comes to me for sex."

"Excuse me?" Raven's head snapped back as she stared at him.

Charger reached around her and opened the door. "I have things to make up to you for and you were right to tell me no sex. It would have just gone back to where things were before."

Okay, this was freaking her out. Was he reading her mind? No, impossible. She was closed off. "Who are you?" Slipped out of her mouth as she stared wide eyed at him.

He chuckled as he walked around her but stopped and cupped her chin. "But I will warn you if you go to anyone else for sex or blood, I will kill the son of a bitch. No questions asked." Charger gave her a hard kiss before he walked out of her bedroom and out the front door.

Raven stood staring at the door confused. "What in the hell just happened?" She asked hoping someone or something would clue her in because she was stumped, and nothing ever stumped Raven.

CHAPTER 10

Raven walked into Dawn Breakers looking around. She was still confused with what happened between her and Charger. Never had he walked away from her like that. He clearly had wanted sex but walked away. She should be relieved, but she wasn't. She was confused and well, sexually frustrated. Damn him and damn her for being a slut where he was concerned. She snorted to herself at her thoughts. Of course, her eyes scanned the room for him, but she didn't spot Charger. Instead, she saw Sid and Lana by the bar. Heading that way, she smiled when her eyes found Stanley waving enthusiastically at her.

"Hey." She said leaning against the bar next to Lana.

"I was wondering if you were coming." Lana smiled at her as Raven gave Sid a nod. "I hear congratulations are in order. Would have loved to have seen you kick ass today."

"Thanks." Raven grinned. "It was definitely a team effort. If truth be told Katrina was the star of the show. Is she here?"

"They are supposed to be." Lana replied, then waved at Pam and Duncan who headed their way.

Pam gave Raven a tight hug. "I knew you would come out on top today." Pam pulled away smiling up at her. "Duncan told me all about it."

Raven grinned down at Pam. She and Pam had a special relationship. She didn't know what it was, but Pam reminded her of Tracy in many ways. "Thanks." She said, noticing Pam wasn't squinting as bad tonight as she usually did. "Is your eyesight getting better."

"A little bit." Pam smiled. "It's slow, but there is improvement. Slade is having me take more of Duncan's blood. He also gave me eye exercises that is helping."

"That's great, Pam." Raven hugged her again. Sometimes Raven was surprised by her own actions. She had never been a hugger, but since meeting the Mates that's all she ever seemed to do. Damn, she was getting soft. "Where's Daniel?"

"He's back at the compound. Said he had things to take care of and that this wasn't really his scene." Pam chuckled, but Raven saw the shift of worry in her eyes. "Duncan said he did really good today."

"We wouldn't have made it if it wasn't for him." Raven admitted with a nod. She felt for Pam, she really did. Being a mother watching your child grow at an alarming rate both mentally and physically had to be scary. Not knowing why he was aging or if he would stop. Daniel was special in so many ways, but Raven knew that didn't help ease Pam's fears.

Pam gave her a smile, then patted her arm before turning toward Duncan taking the drink, he was handing her. Not much intimidated Raven, but Duncan did. His quiet strength had you always guessing what he was thinking. Raven was good at reading people, always had been. Working with Demons it was a talent you had better take to or you'd find yourself dead or worse a slave to the bastards. There were times especially during training she would see Duncan staring at her as if trying to figure her out. Yeah, well, good luck with that. She had yet to figure herself out. The only time she had ever seen him smile was when he was looking at his Mate. Raven watched as Pam said something to which Duncan leaned down toward her as he wrapped his arms around her small waist.

That was what she wanted more than anything. A man who cared enough at what she was saying that he would lean toward her as if not to miss a word. Fuck flowers or candy. She wanted to feel...special, needed and...loved. A cynical laugh escaped her lips as she quickly looked away from their intimate moment. Her eyes landed on Charger who was leaning on the other end of the bar with Kane, a beer in his hand as he stared at her.

Their eyes held until he gave her a slow wink as he tipped the beer to his lips, lips she wished was on her body right now. A sensual feeling exploded in her body, every nerve ending tingled making her weave slightly unsteady on her feet.

"I don't like to be hung up on." Susan said putting her hand on her hip looking around. "Especially when there is juicy gossip to be discussed."

Raven jumped glancing down at Susan then around the bar which was now packed with Warriors, Mates, and Guardians. Holy shit how long had she been staring at Charger. Was he now putting her in a trance? She looked his way to see him grinning at her as if he knew exactly what she was thinking. Okay, she really needed to get a damn grip on herself where he was concerned.

She gave him a narrowed glare before turning her attention away from him. Lana's partner Susan had grown on her. The tiny woman acted as if they had been the best of friends for years, when in truth it had maybe been a month since they first met.

"I'm pretty sure I said bye." Raven countered, but Susan wasn't having it.

"No." Susan shook her head. "No. You didn't. Just hung up and left me hanging."

"I didn't leave you hanging." Raven laughed. "There was no…juicy gossip. Ryker lied."

"Dammit. Okay." Susan frowned as if deep in thought while staring at her, then gave a nod. "Well, I'll find you a man. Don't you worry."

Raven watched Susan walk away as if she was on a mission. Her gaze met Lana who was grinning. "She wouldn't."

"Oh, she would and is at this very moment looking for eligible men." Lana chuckled shaking her head. "You will have a man whether you want one or not by the end of the night. She means well…most of the time."

"I hear congratulations are in order." Chantel's voice had her smiling as she turned around. "And I fucking missed it because some Demon decided to possess a human on my watch."

"You definitely missed a show." Raven turned and hugged her. Chantel was a very dear friend and a deadly Guardian who took no shit from anyone.

"With you involved it's always a show." Chantel laughed then pulled away looking Raven over. "You look good girl. Seems the VC is treating you well."

"It's not bad." Raven replied, then looked her friend over as well. Chantel was a beautiful dark-skinned woman with a body that didn't quit. She was also a badass who could use a sword like no one she had ever met. "And you're looking good yourself."

"Always." Chantel said, then grinned. "Damn I miss you. I should hate you for leaving me with dumb bitches, but I don't, and you should feel honored by that."

Glancing to where Chantel's eyes shifted, she saw Sonya talking with Kane and Charger. Her tiny dress was practically showing ass and her tits were smashed together and falling out in a display. A display men walking by were staring hungrily at. Her gaze went to Charger afraid she would see that same look in his eyes, but to her surprise he was staring straight at her. Raven swallowed hard before looking away quickly.

"So, what's up with you and Charger these days." Chantel asked with a cocked eyebrow.

Not wanting to open that can of worms because honestly, she didn't know the answer, she made a pivot on the conversation. "Let me introduce you to a few people."

"Okay, Raven." Chantel chuckled. "I'll let it go for now, but not long."

Ignoring her last comment, she introduced Chantel around to her new team. And of course, everyone fell in love with her. Duncan and Chantel had a long conversation about swords. Raven didn't think she had ever heard Duncan say so many words at one time. It was a little mesmerizing if she was being honest.

"Oh, I love this song." Chantel grabbed Raven and Lana's hands. "Let's go girls. We need to show them how it's done."

Raven's love for dancing shocked a lot of people who thought they knew her. She didn't wear dresses, but she sure could tear up a dance floor. It was something her, Chantel and Tracy always found time to do. Heading to all the popular dancing spots had been a weekly thing for them. It was their time to unwind.

Jill met them halfway there with Angelina and Katrina following. Raven quickly introduced them to Chantel before she let the music flow through her, and she lost herself in the rhythm. A few men had come up to them trying to move in on the action, but then they were suddenly gone. Glancing around she noticed Slade, Adam, Sid, and Blaze all positioned around the dance floor, arms crossed giving any man who even stepped foot on the dance floor a warning sneer. She had to admit it was nice. The only thing she hated about dancing in clubs was that men figured it was their right to try to pick a woman up just because she was dancing. It was such bullshit, but it happened all the time.

"She a friend of yours?" Jill asked with narrowed eyes toward where Slade was standing.

Raven glanced that way to see Sonya dancing a little too close to the handsome doctor. "Nope." Raven replied, then glanced at Chantel with a grin who was also watching Sonya.

"Good to know." Jill said then headed that way.

"Who taught that girl how to dance?" Chantel asked in disgust. "You think we need to help that little slip of a thing out."

"Who Jill?" Raven laughed then shook her head. "Oh, no. Jill can handle herself just fine."

"Hey!" Steve said as he and Mira came dancing toward them.

"You dance?" Raven grinned first at Mira, then at Steve.

"Can you say John Travolta?" Steve said, then did the famous dance move from *Saturday Night Fever*.

"I told you not to do that anymore." Mira rolled her eyes but laughed at Steve's antics.

"Smooth moves." Chantel said to Steve as he continued to dance and dance actually very well. Except for the John Travolta move.

Raven introduced them to Chantel as they continued to dance. Hearing voices raised over the music, she turned prepared as she always was for trouble. Jill and Sonya were in a heated shouting match. Slade stood looking annoyed as hell.

"Oh, shit." Steve sighed as they all stopped dancing. "Who's the chick about to get a beat down?"

"Sonya." Both Raven and Chantel said at the same time. "A Dark Guardian."

"I thought she looked familiar." Steve frowned then cursed when Sonya reached out running her hand up and down Slade's muscular arm. "Shit just got real."

Steve was right, shit did just get real. Before they could get to Jill and Sonya, Jill's hand shot out lifting Sonya by an unseen force. She was then slammed to the dance floor. Within seconds of hitting, she was sliding toward them. Raven actually had to jump over Sonya as she slid by, her dress hiked up showing her ass.

"Goddamn." Chantel whistled looking from Sonya back to Jill who was heading their way cursing at Sonya, but Slade grabbed her by the waist, put her on his shoulder and walked toward the exit. "That little thing is a badass."

"That she is." Raven grinned, then frowned when Sonya started to march past them following Jill and Slade. Raven stepped in front of her. "You need to chill out, Sonya."

"Fuck you, Raven." Sonya growled trying to push her way past her, but Raven wasn't having it. "She is going to pay for this."

"That man is her Mate, her husband." Raven sneered down at Sonya. "She had every right to do what she did and more. I would count yourself lucky it wasn't more. Jill is not someone you want to mess with, Sonya and neither am I. To get to her you will have to go through me."

"Words of a traitor mean nothing to me." Sonya spat taking a step toward Raven.

"Damn, that was harsh." Steve whistled getting a glare from Raven. "Sorry. Continue."

Chantel stepped between them. "Okay." Chantel grabbed Sonya by the shoulders turning her away from Raven. "This is the only time I am going to save your ass from a beating that would be well deserved. Let's take a walk and cool down, Sonya."

Watching as Chantel turned to give her a wink, she rolled her eyes listening to Sonya bitch as they made their way to the opposite side of the club. She had been called a traitor so much it was starting to lose its sharp edge.

"You good?" Lana asked frowning toward where Chantel and Sonya disappeared.

"I'm fine." Raven replied with a frown. "Sonya and I have a history so nothing new there."

A slow song started to play moving them off the dance floor. Her eyes slowly moved to where Charger had been standing to see him still there now talking with Sloan. Once again, their eyes met, and she was the first to look away.

Susan appeared in her vision. "Got a good one for you."

Raven opened her mouth to tell Susan to stop until she saw who Susan was pulling along behind her. Jackson Riley stood with a grin on his face.

"This is the poor girl who has no one to dance with you were talking about?" Jackson chuckled when Raven frowned glaring at Susan.

"Are you telling people that?" Raven hissed at Susan. "What is wrong with you?"

"I'm not telling people that." Susan said, but Jackson cocked his eyebrow at her lie. "Just a few... guys. So, I take it you know each other?"

"Yes, Susan. We know each other." Raven said, then scanned the crowd. "And where is Ryker by the way."

Susan shrugged. "I don't know. Why?"

"Hmmm, guess I'll give him a call and tell him there is a poor lonely girl here who can't mind her own business and needs the distraction of a handsome man." Raven said raising both eyebrows at her. "Two can play at this game, Susan."

"Okay. Fine." Susan pouted looking disappointed.

"Seriously, I appreciate what you are trying to do, but I don't need a pain in the ass man." Raven said, then glanced up at Jackson. "No offense."

"None taken." He tried to hide his grin but failed miserably.

"I get it." Susan said, then bit her lip looking between the two of them. "But you guys do make a cute couple." Susan's grin spread across her face as she took off with a backwards wave, disappearing in the crowd before Raven could cuss her out.

"Sorry about that." Raven sighed. "She means well, I think."

"No worries." Jackson said with his genuine smile. Dammit he was so good-looking and sweet but could turn badass in a heartbeat. What a catch, and yet he wasn't what she wanted. "How about a dance between...friends."

Before Raven could answer Charger's voice broke into their conversation. "Sorry, but this dance is taken as are all her dances."

"Charger." Jackson gave him a nod of greeting then gave Raven a half smile before backing away.

"Jackson." Charger nodded back then took her hand leading her onto the dance floor.

"That was rude." She whispered as he pulled her into his arms.

"Don't care." Charger replied as he scanned the area before looking down at her with a look that curled her toes in her boots. Holy shit, what in the hell was going on and then she realized the last time she had danced with Charger was at Tracy and Jake's wedding. It felt good to be back in his arms. A small piece of the wall she had continued to build around her heart fell away as she laid her head on his chest and just enjoyed the moment because she didn't know if there would be another one. With Charger O'Neil she took these moments and held on to them for as long as she could. What terrified her was she didn't know if that would be good enough because deep down she knew she deserved much more.

CHAPTER 11

Raven walked into the warehouse not in the best of moods. Last night was one of the best nights she remembered having in quite a while. Dancing, laughing with some old and new friends had been exactly what she needed. Jill and Slade had come back after things calmed down. Chantel had sent Sonya on her way. It was just a nice enjoyable evening with Warriors and Guardians mixing together, getting along. She even saw Sloan laughing and slow dancing with Becky. To her surprise Charger had slow danced with her a few more times, and yeah, it was great.

And then after everyone began to depart Charger walked her to her bike, then got on his. He followed her to her place, but didn't get off his bike. When she invited him in, he declined, pulled her down for a very heated kiss and then waited for her to safely disappear inside.

Once he drove off and she knew he couldn't hear her Raven screamed in frustration. Well, if he thought she was going to come begging him for sex, which she would have gladly given up last night without a second thought he had another think coming.

Throwing her stuff on the ground, she pulled out her phone to turn it on silent while she trained or whatever in the hell they were doing here. Last night Sloan had ordered everyone here at seven a.m. sharp. No explanation whatsoever which was Sloan's style. It took some getting used to.

Glancing at her phone she saw a text from Susan.

Call me ASAP!!!!

Getting ready to do just that and hoping it wasn't about a man because if it was, she was going to slowly kill Susan. She frowned when her phone was snatched from her hand and tossed on her bag. "Hey!"

"Get your ass on the mat, Raven." Sloan's tone indicated he didn't want to hear any shit. "Everyone is waiting on you."

Thankfully she had dressed in workout clothes and brought her normal working attire with her. Following Sloan, she noticed that everyone was present and when she said everyone, she meant everyone, all the Warriors, trainees and even the Mates. Daniel and Katrina stood in the middle of the mat. Sloan gave her a light push toward them.

"I'm sure you three are wondering what you are doing here." Sloan started to speak and that's when she noticed Sloan was in workout clothes. Okay, this wasn't good. So not fucking good. "Even though I am very proud of what you three accomplished during the initiation I'm not satisfied that you are truly ready."

"Wait." Raven frowned looked around at all the Warriors then back to Sloan. "What?"

Sloan ignored her. "There was very little hand to hand combat because of how the Hunters decided to take you out. In our line of business everything usually ends up in hand-to-hand combat. We have seen you train, but not against skilled Warriors." A smile broke out on Sloan's face. It was not a smile she had ever seen before and honestly it scared the shit out of her. "We are bringing back a very old tradition starting with you three."

A murmur of excitement came from the older Warriors standing around. Even Damon had a huge grin on his face. Holy shit what was happening. Glancing toward the door she watched as Charger and Kane walked in. Their eyes met briefly before she looked back to Sloan.

"The Gauntlet." Sloan said then rubbed his hands together. "Each one of you will fight each one of us for one minute. If you are still standing the next warrior comes in and so on and so forth. Any questions?"

"Ah, yeah." Raven said looking around at the Warriors. "What order are you coming at us in?"

"You are smart, aren't you?" Sloan laughed as did the rest of the Warriors. Raven didn't answer, just shrugged because she had a feeling what she was about to hear was what she didn't want to hear. "We will start with the trainees who didn't get through the initiation, then VC Warrior ranking starting with the first and ending with me."

"Holy shit on a stick with firecrackers up my ass." Steve whispered loudly, then did the symbol of the cross as he stared at the three of them. When Raven glared his way, he shook his head. "Sorry, but this is a holy shit moment."

"Sounds like fun." Kane grinned and Raven was now glaring in his direction. "Sorry, but it does. Can we join in?"

"Yes." Sloan gave him a nod. "Get dressed. I'm going to give them time to warm up. Five minutes. Katrina you're first. Daniel second and Raven you are last."

"Asshole." She sneered at Kane when he passed to get dressed.

"You love me, and you know it." Kane gave her a wink as he headed to the locker rooms to change.

Raven noticed that Charger hadn't moved but was staring at her. He nodded her over to him. "Tell Katrina to be defensive. All you have to do is survive to the next round."

"Think I'll leave the word survive out of the conversation." Raven said as she glanced at Katrina who was sitting on the floor barely stretching. Her eyes went to Blaze who didn't look happy at all. Dammit, why in the hell was Sloan doing this. They were ready, passed the initiation and now he wanted to add something on and what he was adding on would scare the fuck out of the most skilled Warrior or even Guardian.

"Go on." He nodded toward Katrina. "And Raven. You got this. Just keep your cool, don't get pissed losing your focus and you'll be fine."

Raven nodded, then headed toward Katrina. If there was one thing Raven would listen to Charger for it was fighting. He had taught her everything she knew. She wasn't stupid. And honestly, she really needed his insight for this one. Steve was right, holy shit on a stick didn't even do this situation justice.

Sitting across from Katrina, Raven began to stretch. "We got this Katrina." She tried her best to pump her up, but she knew

Katrina was scared. Where her gifts excelled, her fighting skills faltered. She was getting better, but was she ready for this, no, she wasn't and honestly it pissed Raven off. "All you have to do is be defensive. As long as you are on your feet for the next Warrior, you're good."

Katrina gave her a small smile and nod. "Thanks, Raven." She said then stood up when Sloan called out to everyone. "You're a good friend."

Raven frowned. It was as if Katrina already gave up. Grabbing her she forced Katrina to look up at her. "Dammit, Katrina. You can do this." Raven gave her a little shake. "Listen to me and don't you dare give up. Do you hear me."

Katrina nodded looking a little more confident as she walked into the middle of the mat.

One thing about Raven was she rooted for the underdog. Katrina in this instance was the underdog. If she really thought about it all three of them were, but Katrina the most. Her eyes once again went to Blaze who was staring at her, but Katrina just stared past him. She suddenly knew the real issue.

"Wait!" She called out holding up a finger to Sloan.

"Make it fast Raven." Sloan ordered surprising Raven. She figured he would give her shit.

Raven leaned close to Katrina so no one could hear her. "Blaze will be proud of you no matter what. Do you hear me, Katrina? You can't worry about him. You have to worry about you."

"I don't want to embarrass him." Katrina whispered back and that told Raven she was right. Her fear for her Mate was much stronger than the fear for herself. That was what love really was.

"That man loves you and nothing you ever do would embarrass him." Raven hissed in her ear. "Now focus on what you need to do."

"Come on." Kent called out. "If she's scared get her off the mat."

Raven pulled away from Katrina and pointed straight at Kent. "I will fuck you up, bitch." She looked back at Katrina after glaring at Kent. "You got this."

Moving back Raven knelt on the floor as close as she could so she could yell things out to Katrina. She didn't care if that was against the rules. Until Sloan bitched her out, she was going to guide her through it. One of the trainees stepped in front of Katrina as they waited for Sloan to call for the start.

"When you hear me call switch the next person be ready to go." Sloan ordered. "There will be no breaks. I suggest you three watch your backs. Go!"

Raven watched as Katrina was faced with her first opponent and damn, she was proud. Katrina was doing great. She countered everything and even got a few hits in."

"Switch!" Sloan called out as the next came at Katrina from behind.

"Behind you!" Both Daniel and Raven warned at the same time.

Katrina was too slow and took a hook to the chin. She stumbled but recovered quickly. Both she and Daniel took turns calling out things and Katrina listened while following through. A few times Raven and Daniel glanced at each other like proud parents.

"That's it Katrina you're doing great!" Raven yelled watching as Katrina slipped out of a potential takedown. She was so excited she was practically bouncing on her knees. Katrina had definitely improved.

"Switch!" Sloan called out and Kent flew from the sidelines jumping in the air, then landed, what many in the MMA world called a superman punch, to Katrina's temple. She never saw it coming. She hit the mat hard and didn't move.

"You son of a bitch." Raven scrambled toward Katrina as Jared, Sid and Duncan held Blaze back from Kent. Kane was holding back Daniel who was cussing at the bastard.

Slade slid next to Katrina. "Move." He told Raven who crawled backward to give him more room. She glared at Kent who just stood there staring down at Katrina, then looked her way with a half grin on his face.

"You're mine." Raven mouthed the words which he just cocked his eyebrow at.

It took a while for Katrina to come out of it. Slade had her sitting up with Blaze right there beside her. She watched as the trainees were grinning. She slid next to a now calmed down Daniel. "I don't give a fuck what you do to them but leave some of Kent for me."

"You got it." Daniel said more serious than she had ever heard him.

"Daniel you're up." Sloan called out.

Raven knew that Kent wouldn't be thrown out because survival was the name of the game. Though what Kent did was extreme, so would her payback for Katrina be and she was looking forward to it.

The first trainee was on the mat in front of Daniel, and he didn't look too confident now. As soon as Sloan said go Daniel was all over him until very quickly, he was knocked out on the mat. Jared pulled him off by the feet as the next one came out. The beatdown continued as each trainee was knocked out quickly by Daniel until it was Kent's turn.

Kent decided to try to distract Daniel with trash talk, but it did no good. Daniel toyed with him, to the point Kent was getting so pissed he resorted to calling Daniel a freak only low enough that Daniel and Raven could hear. Glancing at Duncan she noticed he was frowning. Maybe they weren't the only ones hearing what Kent was saying.

Daniel did as promised, only punishing Kent enough that there was plenty of him left for her when it was Raven's turn. She watched and warned Daniel a few times as each of the Warriors took their turn. Not one of the Warriors held back on Daniel, not even Duncan when it was his turn. Ronan actually knocked him down, but Daniel climbed back to his feet and continued taking a beating while getting in a few of his own.

"Switch!" Sloan called out as he walked onto the mat.

In truth this was the moment Raven had been waiting for. She had heard a lot of stories about Sloan Murphy, leader of the VC unit. Now it was time to see if the hype was just that… hype or if he was truly the badass everyone claimed he was.

Daniel wasn't a vampire, or at least he didn't need blood to survive. He healed like a vampire. He had the speed of a vampire and obviously the fighting skills of a vampire. Daniel wasn't even breathing hard, didn't look tired at all and yet he was no match for Sloan. Every time he tried to counter something Sloan threw at him; Sloan came back with something else. It was brutal and yet, Daniel kept fighting. The Warriors began to clap as the round was coming to a close. Sloan spun and kicked hitting Daniel in the jaw. It took him to one knee. Daniel swayed, shook his head, but stumbled to both feet just as Charger yelled time.

Fuck that was brutal, Raven thought to herself wishing now she had gone first. Witnessing this before her turn hurt her confidence a little. Her stomach pitched and on the inside her nerves were out of control, but she knew on the outside she looked calm, cool, and confident.

"You're up." Sloan pointed at her then the mat. "Hope you paid attention."

"So do I." She whispered to herself as she made her way to the center of the mat. Her eyes briefly glanced at Charger who just gave her a nod of encouragement.

"Don't worry. You'll be resting your pretty head on the mat when it's my turn." Kane whispered from behind her.

She flipped him off without even looking behind her. Taking a deep breath, she closed her eyes and began to focus. It wasn't until Sloan's voice called out that her eyes slowly opened. Her whole personality clicked into survival mode, a mode she was most comfortable with. It was her or them and she would be damn sure it was them. A smile formed across her lips as the crazy took over. It was time to let the real Raven out.

CHAPTER 12

The first three trainees were easy, the fourth she played with until she knew Sloan was ready to call out the next one which would be Kent. With the speed that was needed she fell to the ground and scissor kicked the fourth one's legs causing him to fall backwards. Once he hit the ground, she was ready with an elbow to the face knocking him out cold. Her eyes briefly met Charger's who gave her a nod, but also a warning as he looked behind her. This time it was Duncan who pulled the trainee off the mat.

Knowing in her gut how Kent was going to come at her, Raven continued to stare toward Charger. Using every instinct she had she waited patiently. Charger's eyes flickered and she knew the strike was coming. Turning she picked up her leg and kicked out just as Kent was flying at her with the same superman punch, he hit Katrina with. Her foot connected with his stomach sending him across the room as her leg straightened in a kick that she knew hurt like hell.

Hearing murmurs throughout the room she ignored them as she headed toward the bastard who was just picking himself off the ground. With a roar he charged her, but she was ready. Sidestepping she round kicked him square in the face sending his feet over his head as he fell backwards. He didn't get up as quick this time.

Walking over she leaned over him. "Get up, pussy."

With a roar Kent angrily swiped the blood off his face. He came at her with a vengeance, but his anger was on her side. He was sloppy, making mistakes as he swung haymakers toward her. She easily countered and then made contact with her own attacks. Knowing that their time was almost over she had one more move she wanted to finish him with. Grabbing his shirt, she pulled him toward her.

"Next time you ever hurt one of my friends like that I will kill you." She whispered for his ears only.

Before he could respond with something stupid, she reared her head back and head butted him, then pushed his limp body away from her just as Sloan commanded the switch.

And so on it went. Never in her life had she ever had to fight like she was fighting. Every single Warrior she fought from the scary son of a bitch Damon to sweet but badass Jill, Raven felt like her body was going to break at any moment. Steve kept asking if she was okay and apologizing every time he got in a good shot.

When it was Adam's turn, he knew she was exhausted and told her he had read her in order to tell Charger where she was when she was with Lee, her blood donor. That pissed her off enough to give her a second wind. But the exhaustion came back quickly and yet, she kept going. Refused to go down. Or at least stay down. She had gone down quite a few times, once when Bishop hit her with a spin kick to the side of the head. It took her a few seconds to remember where she was and what the hell she was doing. Charger was yelling at her from the sidelines to keep her fucking hands up which was nearly impossible because they felt like lead weights. God, she was so tired.

"Switch." Sloan's voice called out. Raven had no idea how many more were coming for her, but she hoped not many. Bent over she shifted her eyes around to see who was coming next. Only seeing legs, she knew it was Sloan stepping onto the mat.

"Fuck!" Raven swallowed hard and tasted blood at the back of her throat. Her face was swollen, and one eye was almost completely shut which sucked. She would heal, but after a beating like this it would take a while. Good news this was her last minute of misery, bad news…it was Sloan.

Seeing his leg lift she knew a kick was coming and honestly, she didn't think she could take anymore. Instead of sucking it up she tucked and rolled away from the kick. Rolling to her feet she bent in a defensive manner ready for what was to come next. It was time to take the advice she gave Katrina. Defensive and survive.

"You ready to quit?" Sloan goaded her, but she wasn't going to take the bait.

"You going to talk for the whole minute?" She shot back and was surprised when he smiled before turning serious and unleashing hell on her.

Never in her life had she blocked so many punches and kicks. Sloan unleashed on her, but in truth she knew he was holding back. If he wanted to, he could take her out right now, but he wasn't. He was allowing her to defend herself. It wasn't like he was toying with her either. He was testing not only her physical state, but mental state as well.

Sloan faked a punch to her face and when she brought her arms up to protect, he dropped and swept her legs out from under her. Within a second, she was flat on her back looking up to see Sloan with his fist raised. This was it. He had her. No way could she defend in the position she was in.

"Time!" Sloan called out and dropped his fist. "Damn fine job, Raven. I'm fucking impressed and nothing impresses me."

He reached down to help her up, but she swallowed and shook her head. "Think I'm going to stay here for a minute if that's okay, sir." He straightened with a nod then turned to walk away. "Sloan."

Sloan turned looking down at her with a cocked eyebrow.

"Thought Warriors didn't hit women?" Raven said, then smiled through cracked lips.

"The time you were on this mat you were a Warrior." Sloan turned very serious as he stared down at her. "A very worthy Warrior who we are proud to call one of our own. I'll send Slade over."

Kane knelt down next to her. "Damn, Raven." He looked her over. "You look like shit."

"Fuck you, Kane." She wheezed trying not to laugh. "And that leg kick you got me with was a pussy ass move."

"Worked didn't it." Kane gave her a wink then stood just as Charger knelt down beside her.

"Is Daniel okay?" Raven tried to lift her arms, but they weren't cooperating.

"Slade is with him now." Charger frowned not looking happy at all. "He'll be fine. Katrina is okay."

"Please tell me he looks as bad as I do." Raven snorted, then groaned when the action hurt. "I think a rib is broken."

"Dammit, Raven." Charger growled then glanced behind him before looking back at her. "Slade is coming. Was this really worth it?"

Raven thought for a long minute as she stared up at Charger with her one good eye. "At this moment, maybe not, but tomorrow, yeah it will be totally worth it. I think." She chuckled, the moaned.

Understanding crossed his face as his frown softened. Getting her ass kicked proved she was worthy. Proving herself came naturally to Raven because she always had to do it. Right now, laying here like a pussy wasn't proving anything though.

"I need to get up." Raven said, not sure how she was going to accomplish that.

Charger went to pick her up, but she stopped him. Seeing Kent and the other trainees looking her way she glanced back at Charger. "Just give me a hand up." Raven's eyes pleaded with him. She noticed he also looked toward the trainees before reaching down clasping her hand and helped her to her feet. He stood close to her but didn't touch her. He was just there in case she needed him, and her chest tightened at the thoughtfulness of that action.

"You shouldn't move until I've examined you." Slade walked over with a chair setting it down next to her.

She started to sit down, but her ribs protested. She sucked in the pain but looked at Slade. "I think I'd rather stand if that's okay?" She tried to straighten, but that didn't seem to work out either. "Don't want to appear weak or anything." She tried to tease which was her go to when what she really wanted to do was cry. She hated to cry and never cried in front of anyone...ever.

"Ribs?" Slade frowned waiting for her to answer.

"Yeah, I think so." She nodded touching them to show him exactly where the really bad pain was.

"And I don't think anyone will ever think you are weak." Slade said with a half grin. "Damn good job out there, Raven."

"Thanks." She whispered then bit her lip as Slade felt around her ribs. A hiss of pain escaped her mouth, but she held the rest back.

"Nothing is displaced, which is good." Slade said stepping back. "Anything else hurting. Your head. Are you seeing double?"

Raven actually laughed. "My fingernails hurt if that tells you anything, but nothing that won't soon heal. My vision is fine."

"When was the last time you fed?" Slade lifted her chin checking her pupils.

"Today." Charger answered for her.

"Good." Slade nodded. "It probably won't hurt for you to feed again. You have bruising upon bruising so that is going to take time to heal. The ribs should be better by tonight. If not call me. You may need x-rays. I wish I could give you something for the pain, but as you know nothing will work for you. Get some Epsom Salt and soak in it. It will help even us vampires."

"I will." Raven said, then glanced at Charger. "Can you take me home? I don't think I could ride if I wanted to, and I really don't want to."

"Planned on it anyway." Charger replied then looked at Slade. "Is there anything I should watch for?"

"Vomiting of blood." Slade said, looking her over again. "And if her pain starts getting worse or her vision becomes blurry suddenly. I want a call ASAP."

Charger nodded. "I'm going to get one of the cars. I'll be right back."

"Damn, you look like hell." Daniel informed her as he passed Charger who was on his way out.

Both of Daniels eyes were swollen, one almost shut like hers. His face was bruised, cut and seeping blood. "Have you looked in a mirror?"

Daniel laughed, then groaned. "Don't make me laugh." Daniel grimaced. "Feels like I've been hit by a semi."

Glancing around at the Warriors she chuckled. "We have." She snorted, then groaned herself. "Followed by a train." She noticed Becky and Sloan in a heated conversation. Their voices were raised, but she couldn't hear what was being said.

"We make a good team." Daniel said as he touched his swollen eye.

"Yes, we do." Raven said absently still watching Becky and Sloan. She also noticed other Mates looking angry. "Hey, what's going on over there."

Daniel glanced that way. "Mom is pissed off at dad for participating."

"Participating?" Raven frowned and even that action hurt. "Well, I guess I can see her point. You are her son. I'm sure that was hard to watch."

Daniel laughed. "Not because of me, but because of you. She said they went too far."

She watched Becky shaking her head, then pull away from Sloan when he tried to stop her from leaving. "Seriously?"

"Yeah, they are all pretty pissed off about Katrina also." Daniel chuckled shaking his head. "Guess they don't think you girls are cut out for the Warrior world."

"I know better than that." Raven said, then slowly headed toward where Sloan followed Becky out the door. She did her best not to moan with each step. She slowed next to Katrina. "You good?" She asked Katrina who just nodded. "Good, come on."

Raven grabbed her hand as she continued toward the door. Damn by the time she got out there they'd be gone. The door felt like it weighed a thousand pounds, but she managed to open it. Seeing Becky angrily stomp away from Sloan she tried to hurry that way, but knew she wasn't going to make it.

"Becky!" She called out. Sloan turned to glare at her, but she ignored him. Becky stopped looking at Raven over her shoulder. "Please don't make me come to you."

Becky turned and walked toward her. Charger pulled up getting out of the car frowning at her. "I told you I'd be right back." He didn't look happy to see her outside.

"Yeah, I know." Raven said, then looked from Becky up to Charger. "Can you go get the Mates for me."

"Ah, sure." Charger said sounding as confused as he looked. "Can I ask why?"

"I'd rather you didn't." Raven said, her cracked and swollen lips hurt like hell, and she had already talked too much. She only wanted to say this once.

Charger left and within minutes she was surrounded by the Mates and their Warriors. "What you witnessed tonight is something that had to be done." Raven said as loud as she could through her cracked lips.

"No, I don't believe it did." Becky spoke up searching Raven's face. "What I witnessed was brutal and uncalled for."

"With all due respect you're wrong. If any of you are angry with your Mate for what happened tonight, you are also wrong." Raven looked at each one of them in the eye. "No one forced me to become a Dark Guardian and absolutely no one forced me to become a VC Warrior. That was my decision."

"You were beaten." Tessa said with an angry scowl. "And I for one do not condone a woman being beaten. I lived that life once."

"I was tested, Tessa." Raven corrected her. "There is a big difference and until people see that I will have to continue to prove myself. Not one of you, other than Pam, is angry that Daniel went through the gauntlet…are you?"

When no one said anything proving her correct, Raven sighed.

"One day I am going to be paired with one of your Mates. You better hope I can take a hit. You better hope I can get knocked down and get back up because his life may depend on it." Raven glanced at each of them again. "Sloan was right. During the initiation we were not tested at all in hand-to-hand combat. Tonight, we were, and I am damn proud of what I accomplished."

"After more training I hope to be able to go through it once again. Make it to the end of the gauntlet." Katrina spoke up. "This is also what I have chosen, no one forced me to go onto that mat. I did that on my own free will and I will do it again when I'm ready."

"Sloan has every right to make sure we are ready to face the evil out there and to keep each other safe. If someone is not ready that could mean the life and death of your loved one. So instead of being angry at them, be proud of what we accomplished tonight." Raven said realizing she really needed to lay down for a minute. Her legs started to shake, but she'd be damned if she collapsed after giving this little speech. "Being a Guardian or Warrior is not for everyone, but it's all I know, and I will die for every single one of these men who tested me tonight."

"Raven we are proud of you, but it's just..." Becky searched her face as her sentence faded off.

"It's all I know, Becky." Raven tried to give her a smile, but failed because it hurt too damn much. "If I didn't have this, I would have nothing. I look like hell now and the pain is not... pleasant, but I would step back onto that mat again right now if that meant keeping my unit and those around me safe."

"Come on, let's get you home." Charger whispered taking her arm.

Raven nodded just as every Warrior who was out there thumped their chest as she passed them. She knew it was their way of showing her respect and she appreciated it more than they would ever know. Fighting for respect of her peers was something she battled with all her life and for it to be freely given was something she didn't take lightly.

"Raven." Sloan called out.

Turning only her head she looked his way. "Yeah?"

He thumped his chest and bowed his head. When he looked up, he smiled. "Nice headbutt."

This time Raven did manage a smile as she let Charger help her to the SUV. Once there she glanced behind them. Not seeing any of the trainees she looked up at Charger. "I don't think I can get in myself."

"I've got you." He said picking her up gently and putting her carefully in the seat.

Laying her head back she looked out the window. Everyone was going inside except Katrina who stood staring at her with the saddest look on her face. Raven knew that look. Had worn it so many times. Katrina lifted her hand in a wave just as Charger got in the SUV and started it. Raven forced herself to lift her hand and wave back. She watched as Blaze walked up and put his arm around Katrina, then turned headed toward the warehouse. Katrina looked over her shoulder at her before looking away. It was at that moment Raven committed herself to help Katrina be the best fighter the VC had ever seen.

CHAPTER 13

Charger drove as carefully as he could, but it seemed like every pothole in the road he hit. Rage consumed him each time he heard a moan of pain from her. His hand tightened on the wheel to the point it was hampering his driving.

Every hit she took tonight he had felt as if it was his body taking the beating. It took everything he possessed not to run out there and block every kick, punch or leg sweep just so she didn't have to absorb the pain. He hadn't. He had remained where he was watching what was happening unfold. He was so fucking proud of her that his throat had tightened into a knot.

Stopping at a red light he glanced over at her. Her head was leaned back against the headrest, her eyes were closed. Even with the bruising and swelling she was beautiful.

"You still with me?" Charger asked making light of the situation because Raven wouldn't want it any other way.

"For the moment, but if we're being honest if I died right now, I wouldn't mind it." She said shifting her body with a grimace of pain.

The light turned and he took off careful not to jerk her. "We're almost there." Charger informed her, but she only mumbled a reply. "Listen, I'm proud of you. You did good. Kane had a shiner for about a half an hour. Bishop had a bloody nose. Steve had a welt on his forehead from the knee smash you did. None of them came out of their minute without some sort of injury."

"Good." Raven mumbled enough that he could understand her. "I know any one of them could have taken me out if they really wanted to, but I made it damn hard for them to do it. My goal was to stay upright and inflict at least one injury to each of them."

"You succeeded." Charger smiled like the proud trainer that he was. "I still don't think Kent knows his own name. That was one hell of a headbutt."

"He's a dick." Raven lifted her head slowly. "He didn't have to do that to Katrina. He humiliated her on purpose."

"It's the name of the game, Raven." Charger reminded her, but he did agree with her. Kent was a dick who did want to humiliate Katrina and tried to do the same thing to Raven, but failed.

"Yeah, I know." Raven grumbled. "He's still a dick. I'm going to train her. Katrina reminds me of me. She will be ready next time."

Charger thought back to the speech she gave the Mates before they left. Raven had never had it easy in their world and yet, sometimes he had refused to see that. He was so used to treating her as one of the guys and yet, she wasn't. She was a female who confused the fuck out of him.

"Can I ask you something?" He asked as he pulled up to her place and parked.

She looked over at him, one eye swollen shut, the other staring intently at him. "Sure."

"Do you ever regret that I changed you?" Charger turned off the SUV and gave her his full attention.

She sat there for a long moment staring at him. "You've never asked me that before." Raven finally said. "Why now?"

"I should have asked you a long time ago." Charger replied, then shook his head shifting his eyes away from her. "And I don't know why I'm asking now, but I do want to know. Maybe I'm finally realizing how hard this life has been on you."

"No, Charger. I have never regretted you changing me." Raven said without hesitation. "And yes, this life has been hard on me, but not because of what I am now. It's because as a woman I have to prove myself to everyone, even other women over and over again. Tonight proved that. It was an all-out war between the Mates and their Warrior just because of me and Katrina being a part of the gauntlet. Daniel was not even mentioned because he is male."

"I guess I've never understood that." Charger admitted feeling a little guilty.

"And when I do try to be a woman, I'm told that I've handed in my woman card." Raven sighed shaking her head. "It's a no-win situation for me and others like me. I am caught between two worlds. The woman's side and the man's side. I don't belong in either."

"I'm sorry." Charger said and meant it. "I'm sorry that I never took the time to understand that about you."

Raven closed her good eye and took a deep breath. "Thank you." She whispered, then opened her eye. "Now can we please go inside so I can soak. I'm learning that even though I have a high pain tolerance it still sucks."

"Yes." He smiled at her. "Give me your key."

"It's on top of the light by the door." She informed him.

"That's not smart." Charger frowned at her. "What if someone sees you put it up there, Raven."

"I just got my ass beat by seasoned Warriors." Raven said with her usual attitude tone. "I think I can handle someone who wants to break in and steal what little shit I own."

Charger figured she had a point, but still didn't like it. "Get a damn key chain." He opened the door and got out.

"I lose keychains." She mumbled as she started to open the door.

"Wait there." Charger ordered. "Let me get the door open and I'll come back to help you out of the SUV."

"Yeah, okay." Raven sounded relieved.

It was hard to see Raven helpless. It was rare that she ever was. And for her to be so agreeable when he was ordering her around was definitely not like her at all. Seeing the box of Epsom Salt that he asked Kane to get and drop off he picked it up. Grabbing the key where she said it would be he unlocked the door then put the key in his pocket. He refused to put it back in the spot where anyone could easily grab it. Rushing inside he went directly to the bathroom and started running her a hot bath pouring the Epsom Salt in the tub.

Turning he headed back outside and down the steps. Scanning the area because it was second nature for him to look for trouble, his gaze went toward the SUV to see Raven sitting straight up just staring out the front windshield. Something about her silhouette stopped him cold. It was as if he felt her sadness and loneliness slam into him.

Raven had never spoken to him about her feelings until tonight. What she shared with the Warriors and their Mates tonight, he had never heard. She had opened herself up to keep them from feeling distraught for her. He always knew Raven was special, but honestly, that was because of her skills as a Guardian. After so many years spent with her Charger now realized that Raven was special for much more than that and he hated himself for being blind to her Demons.

~

Raven sat in the car waiting for Charger to unlock the door. She stared out the window, her body throbbing with pain, but she felt alive. Pain always did that to her. As much as she hurt sometimes it was a reminder that she was alive. What she stated to the Mates tonight was absolutely true. She would step on the mat and face the challenge again without hesitation.

Slowly she turned her head only to see Charger standing at the bottom of her steps staring at her. Their eyes held and she wondered what he was doing. It had felt strange opening up to him, something she rarely did at least about herself and her feelings. For her to open up in front of people she was still getting to know shocked her also, but in no way did she want people fighting over something she walked into willingly with eyes wide open. Maybe it was time for her to stop keeping herself so closed off and then again maybe she had been hit to many times in the head tonight to be thinking like this.

Charger finally moved walking around to her side of the SUV. Opening the door, he reached in without saying a word and picked her up carefully. He walked with her up the steps. "I have a bath running now. Kane dropped off some Epsom Salt for you."

"Okay." She whispered, then frowned. "Guess I have to forgive him now for that leg kick he got me with."

"Nah, he's still an asshole." Charger smiled heading toward the bathroom. "He bitched about having to go into a store to get it."

"Dick." Raven snorted, because that is exactly what she would expect from Kane. "You can put me down. I can go from here."

Charger hesitated before he slowly lowered her legs to the floor. "Do you want to feed now or after?"

"After." Raven responded testing her weight on her legs. Her ribs were already starting to feel a little better. But Slade was right. She had been hit so many times in the same areas that she wasn't going to heal instantly.

Slowly she put one foot in front of the other and felt a little stronger than she did before. That was definitely a good sign. Maybe after a hot soak and once she fed a little more from

Charger, she would be good as new. Walking into the bathroom she turned to look at Charger. "Thank you." Raven said putting her hand on the doorknob. "You don't have to stay, Charger. I'll be fine. If you have something to do, I can feed from you tomorrow."

"I'm going nowhere, Raven." He reached out and closed the door. "Yell if you need me."

"Thanks." She said as he disappeared behind the now closed door. Shuffling to the mirror she looked at herself and actually gasped at her reflection. She was almost unrecognizable. Some of the bruising was fading, but the swelling was still prominent. Reaching up she poked at her eye. Damn she wished she had her phone to take a picture. Yeah, she was weird like that, but documenting her war wounds as she called them was something she did. Boy, bet the Mates would freak out on that one she thought with a snort.

With a sigh she turned and looked at the tub that was almost overflowing. Shuffling that way she groaned as she reached down to turn off the water. Slowly she tried to lift her shirt over her head, but it just wasn't happening. After trying for several minutes, she gave up. Glancing from the tub that was probably getting cold now to the door she frowned.

"Charger." She called out and within seconds the door opened. Instead of standing there he walked in and closed the door. "I can't get my shirt off." She was thankful he didn't say anything because asking for help was hard for her and she knew he knew it.

Walking over he carefully began to lift her shirt off, but when she cried out trying to lift her arms he cursed. Grabbing the V-neck of her shirt he ripped it straight down the front. "I'll buy you a new one." He said as he continued to undress her.

Once she was naked, he picked her up and walked to the tub. "Let me know if it's too hot." He bent and started to lower her toward the water.

"It's not." She said trying not to react to his hard body against her naked one. Even in excruciating pain she wanted him. "The hotter the better."

He grunted something she couldn't understand as he lowered her into the steaming water. Instantly her muscles relaxed. Without hesitation she sunk down until her head went under and she remained there for a long minute. If this was what heaven felt like sign her up. Breaking the surface, she opened her eyes to see Charger standing above her, his eyes roaming her body before his gaze locked onto hers.

"I'll leave you alone." His voice sounded rough, and he actually cleared his throat. He turned to leave. "Yell when you're done."

"Charger." She called out suddenly not wanting to be alone. He stopped but didn't turn around. "Don't leave."

CHAPTER 14

"Hey, can you guys hear me?" Susan said as she sat in her car outside the shadiest looking bar she had ever seen. There weren't many cars, but people stood around outside smoking and talking. No one seemed to be paying her much attention which was good.

"Susan!" Peter screamed in her ear making her jump.

"Dammit, Peter." Susan put her hand on her chest. "You scared the shit out of me."

"Sorry, but I've been trying to get in touch with you for five minutes." Peter sounded irritated which wasn't anything new. He always sounded irritated. "Are you there?"

"Yeah, I'm here." Susan said trying to slow her heart rate down. "I'm getting ready to go but was waiting to make sure you could hear me."

"Don't you guys think that maybe, just maybe we should wait for Raven or Lana before doing this?" Griffin's voice came over the line. "I mean I don't think any female should go into a bar called the Bung Hole Dive Bar alone."

Susan rolled her eyes hearing Jinx in the background laughing. "I tried to call them both multiple times, left messages and neither of them have called me back. What do you want me to do? Hope we get another lead on this Louis guy next year?"

"We don't even know why in the hell we are looking for him or how dangerous he is." Griffin huffed. "I vote we wait. I just don't think it's a good idea for you to go in there without backup."

"Who in the hell would name their bar the Bung Hole." Jinx was still chuckling.

"A bung hole." Sam joked making Jinx laugh harder. "Get it."

"Good one." Jinx snorted loudly in the earpiece making Susan grimace.

"Will you two shut the hell up." Peter griped. "I agree with Griffin. I say we wait until Raven and Lana are in touch."

"Listen." Susan frowned shaking her head as if they were in the car and could see her. "Who went into shitholes alone to get information before Lana came back? Oh, right. Me. So chill out and keep the line clear. Now, is the camera okay?" Susan adjusted her choker.

"It looks great." Jinx said sounding somewhat serious. Honestly the guy was a wizard on tech stuff, but he was goofy as hell. Shit, he fit right in and was an asset to the team. "Mic is working amazingly. Can hear you cursing us under your breath so we're good to go."

"Good." Susan glanced up to see that everyone had gone back inside the bar. What Peter and Griffin said was true. Raven had never come right out to say what this Louis Maxwell, Jr. dude was all about. What she did know is that he was responsible supposedly with setting them up and killing a lot of men plus the damn Mayor. The cops hadn't done shit with their investigation into Mayor Groper's death so obviously something weird was going on. Any information she could get she was going to get. Taking a deep breath, she opened her car door and stepped out. "Going in."

"Just watch your ass, Susan." Peter said not sounding happy at all. "This fucking bar isn't even searchable. I really don't like this."

"I'm sure Jinx can find it on the internet." Susan shut and locked her door, then headed toward the entrance of the bar.

"That's a negative." Jinx informed her. "Already tried looking up the old Bung Hole and absolutely zero information comes up. Though I didn't try the back-alley internet."

"Back-alley internet?" Peter asked and Susan wanted to know what that was also.

"Yeah, kind of like the Dark Web, but not as sinister. Easier to get into." Jinx informed them. "I'll see what I can find."

Susan had lived in the area her whole life and never knew this place existed, but then again businesses came and went so she wasn't too worried about it. If it made them feel better they could search, but her main goal was to see if her informant was right, and she could get some information about this mysterious Maxwell character.

Opening the door Susan walked into the bar. It took a minute for her eyes to adjust to the dimly lit interior. The smell hit her immediately and it was a smell she couldn't quite put her finger on, but it was horrible. The place definitely lived up to its name with its unwelcoming atmosphere and outdated neon beer signs. Susan didn't make eye contact with anyone. She just headed to the bar and sat down. The stool wobbled underneath her but held her weight.

Glancing behind the bar she saw a woman scantily dressed leaning against the counter behind her that was lined with alcohol bottles, her arms were crossed, tattoos adorned every part of skin that was exposed which was quite a bit. But what really caught Susan's attention was that she wore sunglasses. It was so dark in here that Susan could hardly see anything. It was very odd. Actually she was getting odd vibes and that usually meant trouble.

"Bitch, you got a customer." A man's voice from the end of the bar yelled out. Everyone started laughing as the woman pushed off the counter and came toward her. "Do your damn job or we will find someone else that will. Actually, this pretty little blonde would do just fine here."

The man stood from the barstool walking toward her. He was handsome in a dark sleezy way. "Oh, me." Susan said pointing to herself trying to act the clueless part. "No, I'm just passing through and thought I'd stop for a cold drink."

The man sat down at the stool next to her. "Is that so?" He said, then made a clicking noise with his mouth. "We don't get many people just passing through since we are down a dirt road going nowhere."

Shit. Okay, that was definitely a fuck up on her part. What in the hell was wrong with her? She was usually on her game, but something about this place just didn't feel right. She didn't feel right, and that God awful stench was distracting her.

"Took a wrong turn." Susan tried to cover her blunder up with that weak ass excuse. Dammit.

"What can I get you?" The woman behind the bar asked and her voice had a robotic tone to it.

"Did you hear that?" The man next to her yelled out to the others in the bar. "She took a wrong turn."

As he was saying this the woman's mouth was moving, but Susan couldn't understand her. The glasses slid down her nose as she bent closer to Susan. Her eyes were solid black under the glasses. "Get out!" The woman's harsh whisper penetrated Susan's ears sending alarm bells going off inside her brain.

"Fuck!" Jinx's voice broke through those alarm bells. "Get the fuck out now! Susan get out!"

Susan stood quickly, but before she could turn the man grabbed her arm spinning her around. "Going somewhere?" The smile that spread across the man's face was full of evilness. His eyes had turned black with red rimming the pupils.

"Apparently not." She responded dropping the clueless girl routine for her normal smartass personality. "I will tell you that if I'm not accounted for in thirty minutes this place will be crawling with the biggest badasses you've ever seen."

The whole room was silent for only a second before it erupted in laughter and that's when she noticed every single person in there had the same evil eyes as the man who wouldn't let her go. She just hoped that her team was still connected and working on a way to get her out of this mess.

~

*R*yker's food had just arrived when his phone rang. Deciding to let it go to voicemail he cut into his steak. Today had been busy as fuck. All he wanted to do was eat and relax for a minute before he finished his shift. He had missed out on the gauntlet for Katrina, Daniel, and Raven earlier, but work called. Sloan had them rotating shifts with the Guardians. It was taking some of the workload off them, but not enough. Though honestly Ryker didn't mind too much. He liked to stay busy.

His phone rang again and again he let it go to voicemail. Taking a drink of his beer he cursed when his phone started again.

"Fuck!" He hissed grabbing it out of his pocket. He didn't recognize the number. It stopped, but started again. "This better be fucking important." He answered.

"Ryker!" A male voice said on the other end sounding panicked.

"Who is this?" Ryker frowned not recognizing the voice.

"It's Griffin." The man said. "Susan is in trouble. She needs help and no one is picking up their fucking phones."

Ryker stood, pulled out his wallet dropped a hundred plus on his plate and headed for the door.

"Sir, was something wrong with your food." The waitress called out, but he didn't respond. "Sir?"

"Where is she?" Ryker demanded heading toward his bike.

"We didn't know." Griffin said, his voice erratic. "She was following a lead and—"

"Where the fuck is she?" Ryker got on his bike and started it up.

"It's called the Bung Hole." Griffin replied quickly. "It's a dive bar down off—"

"I know where it is." Ryker hung up with a curse. The question was how in the hell did she know where it was? No one other than Demons, Demon hunters such as the Guardians and Warriors knew of the place. "Fuck!"

Taking off he made himself ready to face whatever he was about to face. Demons were tricky fuckers, but as a Warlock he had many dealings with them unfortunately. He knew how to fight them, kill them, and keep his own soul, or what was left of it, intact. Susan was fresh beautiful meat that they were going to devour if he didn't get to her in time.

Rage spurred him on as he ran red lights, jumped medians, and cut off traffic to make sure that didn't happen. Seeing the cutoff, he slid sideways onto the dirt road. Slowing he came to a complete stop got off his bike and grabbed his long duster with his weapons inside. Weapons he was going to need for this fight.

Walking toward the bar he checked to make sure his amulet was around his neck, spoke a quick protection spell just as he burst through the door. In one sweep he assessed the place, knew where everyone was as his eyes gazed past Susan's shocked expression.

"Let her go." His head snapped to the bastard who was standing behind Susan with his hands on her shoulders. She was sitting in a chair with a man kneeling in front of her. He slowly stood up then faced Ryker.

"Says who?" The man said, his voice sounding pleasant and yet, had such an evil undertone it was deceiving. Well deceiving to most, but not Ryker. He knew this fucker's type. He was a trash Demon doing work for more important Demons. He also liked to toy with humans which pissed Ryker off because this time the motherfucker picked the wrong human.

"I won't ask again." Ryker announced, his eyes moving toward a man who was slowly making his way toward him. "One more step and you die."

With lightning speed Ryker reached into the front pocket of his jacket and grabbed his throwing star doused in Holy water. With precision he threw it making a perfect hit in the man's forehead. He screamed as black veins splintered across his skin and fell to the floor.

"He didn't take a step." One man cried out the dumb statement.

"I lied." Ryker replied with an evil smile of his own. "Who's next?" He knew without a doubt the only way he was walking out of here with Susan was if every single one of these bastards were dead.

Within seconds they shed their human forms, grotesque figures appeared in their place hissing as they tried to surround them, but Ryker was too fast and too good for these small-time Demons. Once his stars were gone, he pulled out his knives and began his attack. Soon the bar floor was littered with dead Demons, the best kind.

"Forgot one." The man who thought he was Satan himself said as he held a wicked looking blade to the side of Susan's neck.

"No, I didn't" Ryker said cocking an eyebrow at him. "I just saved the dumbest for last."

With a speed unseen by the human eye Ryker threw one knife backhanded hitting the man right between the eyes. The Demon released Susan who scrambled out of the chair as Ryker passed. His eyes spotted the blood on the side of her neck and rage filled him. Grabbing the man by the throat he pulled the knife out of the Demon's forehead and began to chant. Where his hand held the man's throat the black veins, what they called the Demons' death, began to spread up his face. Ryker squeezed tightly as he finished the chant then threw him against the wall where he seemed to stick then slide down until his limp body hit the floor.

"Holy shit!" Susan said as she looked around, then up to him with wide eyes.

"Holy shit?" Ryker growled as he glared down at her. "That's all you have to say is Holy shit. How about telling me what in the fuck you are doing here alone? No, not even alone. Just here period."

"Well, ah, see." Susan started, but a noise from behind the bar had him pulling her behind him as he spun with his knife poised to strike. "No! She warned me. Told me to get out. I think she's human, but they did something to her."

"Possessed." Ryker frowned walking toward the woman. He pulled her sunglasses off and cursed. He turned to look at Susan. "Exactly what they were getting ready to do to you."

"Oh, shit." Susan's eyes widened as she stared into his.

"Yeah, that's one way to put it." Ryker said shaking his head. "You and I are going to have a long talk, Susan. A very long talk."

CHAPTER 15

Raven didn't know how long she soaked, but she was feeling much better. The water was cooling, but she wasn't ready to move yet. Charger had stayed and was sitting on the floor with his back against the wall. They hadn't talked much, both of them lost in thought and yet, it was nice to have him there. She didn't feel as lonely.

"Is my face looking a little more normal?" Raven asked glancing toward Charger who had his eyes closed. They opened and his golden eyes met hers. "I think the swelling has gone down some around my right eye. At least I can see better."

Charger nodded. "It does look like the swelling is going down. How do your ribs feel?"

Shifting a little bit, she hardly felt any pain. "I think better."

Standing Charger came closer then knelt on the floor. He bit into his wrist. "Go ahead and feed a little bit. That should help even more."

Sitting up, she grabbed his wrist and brought it to her mouth. Their eyes met as she took his blood. She knew she didn't need a lot because she had just fed from him. Even for them too much blood could be a bad thing. After a few long pulls she removed her mouth then licked his wounds so they could heal.

"Thank you." She said noticing every time he looked at somewhere she was bruised, he frowned looking angry. "I've been injured before, Charger. Why are you looking so angry?"

Charger stood again and went to grab a towel. Walking back toward her, he reached out his hand to help her up. She stood and he wrapped the towel around her, then lifted her out of the bathtub before he said anything. "You have never been hurt like this." He set her on her feet. "It's very hard for me."

"Hard for you?" Raven managed a grin trying to lighten the mood. "You should be in my skin."

Charger didn't laugh, didn't even smile. Instead he cupped her chin with his large hand and brought her face up to his. "I don't think you know how difficult it was for me to watch. Even though I know your skills I am a man watching a woman take a beating." She started to open her mouth, but he put his thumb against her lips. "I'm not saying you aren't worthy because you are a woman, Raven. It's just that you are *my* woman."

They stood staring at each other, their mouths coming close to each other and then his phone rang. Neither of them moved. "You going to answer that?" Raven whispered as it continued to ring.

"Fuck!" Charger reached into his back pocket pulling out his phone. "Yeah." He growled into the phone.

Raven stepped back and walked to the mirror. Sure enough her face was healing. It was far from looking normal, but it definitely looked much better. She moved her body, lifting first one arm and then the other relieved that the pain was subsiding. Her limbs didn't feel like dead weights now and she felt somewhat refreshed from soaking in the tub. She was also sure that Charger's blood had a lot to do with her quick healing.

"What in the fuck was she doing there?" Charger said into the phone gaining her attention.

Raven turned to see Charger staring at her.

"Yeah, okay." Charger said not looking happy. "I'll be there as soon as I can."

"What?" Raven frowned as soon as he hung up.

"That was Ryker. I've got to go. Do you want me to call someone to stay with you until I get back?" Charger looked her over as if checking how she was healing.

"What's going on, Charger?" Raven knew Charger well enough that he was not telling her something because he didn't want her to know. "You said what the fuck was she doing there? Who is she?"

"Susan went to a Demon dive bar to follow up on a lead." Charger sighed reluctantly. "One of her team got a hold of Ryker. He took the whole bar of Demons out."

Remembering the text from Susan right before the gauntlet when Sloan took her phone had Raven cussing. "Dammit." Raven turned and walked out of the bathroom heading toward her bedroom. "I'm going with you."

"Raven, you need to rest." Charger followed her out then almost ran into the back of her when she stopped suddenly and turned around.

"I'm going with you or on my own." Raven gave him her 'I'm not asking' look. "Wait until I'm dressed or don't. Either way I am going. She was there because of me. The lead she was following was because of me."

"What lead?" Charger frowned as if he already knew.

Raven turned to look at Charger once she was in her room. "You already know what lead, Charger. If that son of a bitch is responsible for Tracy's death, I will find him or maybe he will find me first, either way the bastard is dead." She said with little emotion because honestly if she showed any right now, she might breakdown and she couldn't do that. "Just because you and my father have secrets you are keeping from me doesn't mean I'm not going after the bastard."

She went to slam the door, but he stuck his boot out and stopped it, then pushed his way into her bedroom. "We were trying to keep you safe, dammit." Charger hissed his eyes narrowing. "What do you not understand about that?"

"I don't want to get into this with you, Charger." Raven dropped the towel not caring that he was seeing her completely naked. He had seen her naked many times now. Slipping on a pair of panties and a bra, she grabbed a shirt and slipped it on. She did it a little too fast causing her to cry out in pain. Yeah, she wasn't totally healed yet.

"Stop before you hurt yourself more." Charger ordered, but she ignored him. "Will you stop and listen to me for a second."

"Are you going to tell me everything because if not then no, I won't give you a second." She grabbed a pair of jeans off the dresser and pulled them on slower than she usually did. Next was her boots and that was going to be a real bitch. Grabbing a pair, she sat on the edge of her bed and bent over to pull them on. Dull pain radiated through her ribcage, but she just bit her lip and kept going.

"You are the most hardheaded person I've ever met." Charger knelt in front of her, knocked her hands out of the way and laced up her boots for her.

"Right back at ya." Raven shot back then started to stand but he stopped her.

"We thought he was dead, Raven." Charger explained looking her directly in the eyes. "We never found the bodies."

"Then you both lied to me." Raven frowned feeling a tinge of betrayal. "I killed his pregnant wife, Charger. Did you not think that if he was alive, he wouldn't come after me to revenge them? I had a right to know that you *thought* he was dead. Instead, you both told me he *was* dead, and I believed you. There's a big difference between the words thought and was. If I had known he may still have been alive I would have hunted him, but now I am being the one hunted. Worse, anyone close to me is being hunted. If that explosion that took Tracy's life is because of me, I will never be able to forgive myself or you."

"Have you forgotten how mentally fucked up you were?" Charger's voice deepened. When she didn't answer he leaned close to her face. "I do, Raven. I remember exactly how fucked up you were."

"She and her child were innocent in all of it, so yeah, I remember it fucked me up. How could it not, but that still didn't give either of you the right to lie to me." Raven scooted across the bed and stood. "Let's go. I don't want to talk about this anymore. My goal now is to find the bastard and take him out before he can hurt anyone else that is innocent in this mess."

Raven walked out of the bedroom searching for her phone. Cursing she turned toward Charger ready to ask him if he had grabbed it from the warehouse. He was already holding her phone out to her. Taking it she checked her messages and cursed again. She had so many missed calls from Susan, Griffin, Peter and Sam. Grabbing a leather jacket out of the closet she headed toward the door, the conversation they just had going through her head. They never found…wait a minute. Slowly she turned toward Charger. "Did you say…bodies?"

Charger didn't say anything, just stared at her.

"Oh, my God. You said bodies." Raven stumbled back in shock. "You never found Delilah Maxwell's body?"

"There is no way she could have survived the fall from the balcony, Raven." Charger countered, and it was weak. Very weak. "Everyone was concerned for you. Once I got there, we found nothing."

Raven stood there absorbing everything she had just learned and honestly, she didn't know how to feel. So many emotions were flowing through her pain that she just wanted to scream but didn't.

"I will never apologize for trying to keep you safe." Charger's voice broke through her scattered thoughts. "Hate me if you must, but I will not apologize for what was decided that night."

Raven squeezed her eyes shut for a second until pain from her still somewhat swollen eye had her opening them again. Slowly she turned. "It wasn't your decision to make." Raven said, then nodded as if accepting what he said. "Let's just find the son of a bitch before he hurts anyone else. What's done is done."

Grabbing the keys off the counter Charger followed her out of the house to the SUV. He opened the door for her watching her closely. "Are you sure you're up to this?" Charger said, then sighed when she gave him a narrowed look. "Just hours ago you could hardly move, Raven."

"And now I'm moving just fine." Raven countered, then curbed her attitude because he did look concerned. "Really, I'm okay. I'm a vampire, remember. I just have a few sore spots left and still look like I've been in a fight, but I'm good."

Charger shut her door, then walked around the front of the SUV and got in, started it up and took off. Her phone which was on silent started to vibrate. Grabbing it out of her jacket pocket she saw Lana's name flashing.

"Hey." She answered hoping Lana had some news.

"Have you talked to Susan?" Lana asked sounding worried.

Raven put her on speaker. "I've got you on speaker. And no, I haven't. We are on our way to where she's at. Where are you?"

"Waiting for Sid." Lana said, then cursed. "I did talk to Peter. He said that she went after a lead alone when she couldn't get ahold of us. Call me as soon as you know something if I'm not there yet. Sid should be here any time. I wanted to go ahead and head out, but he doesn't want me going without him. I swear I'm going to kick her ass when I see her. She promised me she wouldn't do this shit alone anymore now that we are a team again."

"I'll hold her while you kick her ass." Raven added not liking the idea that Susan was known to do stuff like this. It was too dangerous. Louis was too dangerous. Especially for a human because of the Demon company he was known to keep. "But yeah, I'll keep you informed."

"Thanks." Lana said, then hesitated for a brief second. "Raven, how dangerous is this guy?"

Raven glanced over at Charger who was already looking her way. "Very."

Hanging up she sighed, then cursed long and loud. "Damn Susan. What in the hell was she thinking? What did Ryker tell you?"

"He found her in a Demon dive bar." Charger said, his frown prominent on his face.

"Her informant obviously didn't tell her that detail." Raven hissed shaking her head. "Well at least we can question a few of them to see if Louis is involved with any of them."

"Yeah, don't think that is going to happen." Charger said giving her a quick glance. "Ryker took them out."

"The whole bar?" Raven's eyes widened. That was impressive. Demons were hard to kill when in groups. They were sneaky fuckers who didn't fight fair. You had to know what you were doing and obviously it seemed Ryker did. "Damn, sounds like he'd make good Guardian Material."

CHAPTER 16

Susan leaned against her car where Ryker put her and told her to stay. "As if I'm a dog." Susan snorted giving him a narrowed glare which he didn't see because he was busy talking on the phone.

Kicking at a rock, she pushed off the car, but stopped when Ryker turned to give her a warning gaze. With a huff she fell back against the car again. Glancing around she noticed the cars in the parking lot. Did Demons need cars? Couldn't they just beam themselves to wherever they wanted to go. Any movie she ever saw Demons didn't drive cars. The thought came to her suddenly as she glanced toward Ryker who was walking back into the bar.

Her eyes scanned the parking lot finding the nicest one. Biting her lip, she eased off the car again. Her informant said that this Maxwell guy was associated with this place. He didn't know how, but word on the street was just that. So, of course, Susan went with it. Taking another look toward the bar she quickly and as sneakily as she could made her way toward the sleek black sporty looking car. She didn't know what kind of vehicle it was, but it looked expensive and the asshole who held the knife on her was dressed just as expensive. Clothes she knew, cars not so much.

She had no clue if any of those men was the man Raven was hunting, but she sure as hell was going to try to find out. Maybe one of these cars held the answer. Reaching the car undetected she crossed her fingers as she tried the door handle. Susan screamed as the alarm blared throughout the silence of the parking lot.

"Fuck. Fuck. Fuck." She cursed as she stood there guilty as hell. Ryker came busting ass out of the bar, his eyes black as night landing right on her.

"What are you doing?" Ryker growled as he stomped her way.

"Nothing." She lied and when he gave her a cocked eyebrow glare she sighed. "Okay, I was doing something. I'm a cop."

"Was a cop." He grunted as he reached inside the open window hitting the unlatch button. Walking around he popped the hood, did something and the alarm went silent.

"A damn good cop." Susan crossed her arms peeking around to see what he was doing, but he slammed it making her jump backward. "And now since you went Rambo on their asses I don't know if one of them was who I was looking for."

"Rambo?" Ryker frowned at her looking confused.

"Yeah, you know…Rambo up the place." Susan rolled her eyes when he still looked confused. "Don't you guys watch television?"

"No." Ryker replied looking up the dirt road then back at her.

"Storm in and shoot the place up killing everything in sight." Susan continued trying to get him to understand.

"I didn't use a gun." Ryker said just not getting it.

"Which was actually very impressive." Susan had to admit biting her lip then shook her head to clear it. "One of those guys may have been this Maxwell asshole that was responsible for killing Mayor Groper and those military men. I was going to check the cars to see if I could find any identification since they won't be talking. It's what I do. Look for evidence at the scene of a crime because I'm a cop."

"Was a cop." Ryker reminded her again just as a car came into sight. He stepped in front of her in a protective manner. "Raven can identify when she gets here."

"Oh, so she answered your call, did she?" Susan huffed throwing her hands up in the air. "Wow, just wow."

"Actually, it was Charger who answered his phone." Ryker said with a half grin, then he shook his head as if trying to understand her before he headed toward the SUV pulling up.

"Yeah, good luck with that buddy." Susan snorted under her breath. People have been trying to figure her out all her life.

"What?" He stopped looking at her over his shoulder.

"Nothing." She cleared her throat. "Just clearing my throat."

Ryker's eyes narrowed as he stared at her but remained silent as he turned back toward the SUV. Charger got out of the driver's side just as Raven stepped out.

"This is what happens when you don't answer your phone." Susan started on Raven before she could even shut the door. "I get my ass in a lot of trouble. Where in the…hell happened to your face?" Susan was trying to say where in the hell have you been, but once she saw Raven's battered face her words changed. Not many understood Susan's language other than Lana, but now it seemed Raven did also.

"I'm fine. What in the hell are you doing, Susan?" Raven stomped toward her. "You don't go after leads without backup. That was our promise."

"Ah, you have." She reminded Raven with a tsk.

"I'm immortal." Raven proceeded to remind Susan.

"Are you sure about that? Looks like you're close to death." Susan frowned getting a real good look at Raven the closer she got. Anger filled her as her head snapped toward Charger. "Did that fucker do that to you? I swear to God if he did, I will tear off his pecker and beat him to death with it."

Raven just stared at her then laughed. "No, Charger didn't do this to me." Raven continued to laugh. "Damn for a little thing you sure are…"

"Spunky." Susan filled in the blank when Raven couldn't seem to find the right word to describe her. Once again not many words could describe Susan unless it was strung together with others. So spunky seemed to be the one word that fit.

"Definitely." Raven said, then glanced toward the bar and frowned. "What in the hell were you thinking coming here by yourself. This is a Demon dive."

"Well, didn't know that until I was already in deep shit." Susan frowned then shrugged. "We researched, but it never showed up on any of the searches."

"Demon bars usually don't." Raven informed her. "What were you told that you came here?"

"The informant said that Louis was associated with this place. Gave me directions and well here we are." Susan said, then glanced at Ryker who was still talking with Charger. "Then Rambo over there came in shooting the place up."

"I thought Ryker killed them all." Raven frowned looking confused. "You can't kill Demons with bullets even silver bullets unless they are infused with Holy water."

"Do none of you…immortals even know who Rambo is?" Susan rolled her eyes. "He didn't actually shoot the place up. He used these throwing star things and had knives. I will admit it was pretty damn cool, not that I think death is cool. Well, seeing these assholes die was…"

"Susan." Raven snapped her fingers. "Focus. Did you find out any information?"

"No." Susan sighed. "I went inside, smelled a God-awful stench, but then again look at the dump."

"Demon 101…they stink." Raven gave her that little detail that would have helped greatly about a half an hour ago. "Continue."

"Noted." Susan said just as a motorcycle came roaring down the dirt road. A very handsome man got off the bike and she recognized him. Kane, a dark Guardian. "Damn, are all you immortals good looking." Susan sighed as Kane glanced their way and gave her a wink.

"Susan." Raven warned sounding frustrated. Another one of Susan's many talents. Frustrating the hell out of people.

"Sorry." Susan's gaze returned to Raven. She really wanted to ask what happened to her face since she still hadn't told her, but used her self-control not to. Raven was a badass who could literally kill her without breaking a sweat, so yeah, she needed to focus. "Anyway, I was getting ready to order a drink. This guy all dressed in expensive clothes that did not fit the scene, if you know what I mean, started talking and saying stuff. Nothing important, just being an asshole. But the girl behind the bar came over, said something that I couldn't understand and then when she bent down to repeat it her sunglasses slipped. Which in itself was weird that she was wearing sunglasses because it's dark as Satan's asshole in there. Play on words for the situation clearly intentional. Anyway, her eyes were nothing but black. She told me to get out and not in a 'I don't like you' kind of get out. It was a warning. Just as she said that Jinx started yelling in my ear to get out. He found this place on some web thing he knows about and saw that it was a Demon hangout."

Charger walked over just as she finished. "You want to identify before we dispose or do you want me to."

"No, I'm going to do it." Raven replied with a little edge to her tone as she headed toward the bar with Susan right beside her.

"So, what happened to your face?" Susan inquired hoping to get the scoop.

"Had to fight all the Warriors." Raven said as if she was discussing what she had for dinner.

"All at once?" Susan gasped; her eyes wide as she looked up at Raven. Out of anything Raven could have told her that was not something she was expecting. "Damn."

"One at a time for a minute." Raven replied absently as she stepped around Ryker who was also looking at Raven's face.

"Good job." Ryker gave Raven a nod. "Sorry I missed it."

"Thanks." Raven replied with a grin. "Got a few good shots in myself."

"Okay, what am I missing? You congratulate her for getting battered by a bunch of big ass Warriors?" Susan frowned as she tried to also step around Ryker, but he blocked her way. She tried to step to the other side, but he once again stopped her. "Ah, excuse me."

Ryker only cocked his eyebrow at her, but he didn't budge. They had a staring contest in silence before Charger came to the door.

"Ryker, we need you." Charger said then disappeared back inside.

"Wait here." Ryker ordered giving her a warning look.

"You can't order me around like I'm a dog." Susan growled, then realized she growled....like a dog.

"I'm not kidding, Susan." Ryker said just as Charger yelled for him again. Ryker turned and disappeared inside.

"Neither am I, Ryker." Susan mocked him with a narrowed glance that he never saw. And to think she was crushing on him, thought he was cute and instead he was an overbearing... okay, he was still very cute, and his glances did make her heart speed up. "I'm an idiot." She whispered to herself.

Noticing the door was still open Susan glanced around then took a few of her sneaky steps. Looking inside she saw Kane with the woman from behind the bar. She was sitting in the chair Susan had been sitting in earlier. He had his hand on her forehead while Ryker stood behind her holding her shoulder. Okay, this looked oddly familiar.

The woman began to shake, the chair wobbled underneath her. Kane was chanting something as the woman's black soulless eyes opened wide as did her mouth in a silent scream. Susan's eyes shot to the floor to see the chair start to rise off the ground. Just then an inhuman scream erupted from the woman, she began cursing everyone as spit came flying out of her mouth.

"Holy shit." Susan whispered realizing she was witnessing an exorcism or something pretty damn similar. Her eyes shot to Ryker just as his gaze met hers. His head snapped to the side just as the door slammed in her face sending her backwards almost tumbling down the steps.

She didn't know how long she stood there just staring at the door listening to the most heinous sounds coming from inside the bar, but she finally snapped out of it as a female human cry came from inside. Swallowing hard she back peddled then turned toward her car admitting to herself that maybe just maybe she was out of her element here.

Leaning against her car once again, her eyes went back to the bar. "I really need to get me some Holy water." She whispered absently to herself. "Maybe a cross or three."

A noise from the back of the bar caught her attention. With a frown she slowly straightened, moved sideways to see if she saw anything. Hearing it again she headed that way.

"Bad idea, Susan. Just stay like the good doggie you are." She whispered to herself as she looked at the bar. The door was still closed. They were busy so she would just take a little peek. What would it hurt? Ryker had done a quick sweep of the place, so she wasn't that concerned and yet here she was walking into the unknown giving herself a pep talk. "It's fine. Probably just a racoon, maybe a cute little rabbit. Nothing to worry about."

Turning the corner, she saw something she hoped to never see again. A man was crawling, yes crawling, up the side of the building. Susan had seen some shit working on the police force, even creepy shit, but this just was beyond even her creepy scale. This was just plain fucking creepy times a thousand.

"Crap." She hissed as she reached behind her back. Susan slowly pulled out her gun from her waistband. The man, thing or whatever it was, because let's get real no human could scale a wall like that, hadn't seen her yet. Raising her gun, she aimed just as it was ready to bust through the window it was desperately trying to get to. "Freeze fucker!"

The fucker didn't freeze. Its head snapped toward her as a huge evil grin spread across his face. It looked human, but the eyes gave it away. Nothing, but black. In one leap it jumped from the side of the building and walked toward her as if she wasn't holding a gun.

"I'm not playing asshole." Susan warned standing her ground. Obviously, he wasn't playing either because he kept coming. Knowing she was running out of time she took careful aim and pulled the trigger. The shot hit him square in the forehead. His head snapped back, but he stayed on his feet. Yep, she definitely needed bullets with infused Holy water. This paranormal shit was out of control. She could at least slow him down enough for her to escape. "I tried to warn ya." Susan said as she unloaded her clip hitting him in the chest.

Okay, that plan didn't work. Instead of slowing him down it just pissed him off. Susan turned to run with a scream building in the back of her throat. She felt like a cartoon character when they started to run, but their feet just spun.

"Fuck!" Finally she got traction but she knew it was too late. She felt his hand barely miss her shirt.

Looking up she saw Ryker, Kane, and Charger heading right toward her. Ryker reached her first, grabbing her out of the way by wrapping his arm around her waist as he tossed her back to Kane. He spun nailing the guy with his knife to the throat. Black veins appeared spreading up his face as he also died a gruesome Demon death.

Kane let her go and she sat heavily on the ground, then laid back gasping for breath. A shadow appeared over her. Opening her eyes she saw Ryker glaring down at her.

"What part of stay do you not understand?" He frowned down at her.

"I'm not a fucking dog." She wheezed past dry lips. "I'm a cop. A good cop."

Ryker leaned down enough to get her attention. "Was a cop." He hissed, then cursed as he straightened and walked away.

"Shut up." She hissed back, then closed her eyes trying to get her breathing back to normal.

"Like living on the edge, don't you?" This time it was Raven who was looking down at her.

"Ehh, only when I get bored." Finally she sat up and wiped the sweat from her forehead, then squinted up at Raven. "Who in the hell is this Louis asshole because it's quite obvious he isn't some schmuck that pissed you off one night. It's story time, Raven."

Raven nodded, then held her hand out to help Susan up. Glancing around she saw that Kane was dragging the man to the other side of the bar while Charger stayed close to them. Ryker on the other hand was nowhere to be seen. Just as well since all she seemed to do was piss him off today. Which was probably a good thing. She didn't have time to get involved with anyone especially a sexy vampire Warrior warlock whose voice turned her insides to mush and her... Ryker stood at the top of the hill staring down at her cutting her off in mid thought. Okay, dammit maybe she could make a little time for a sexy vampire Warrior warlock.

CHAPTER 17

Raven leaned against Susan's car waiting for Lana and Sid to arrive. Other Guardians had shown up to help dispose of the Demon bodies and answering all of Susan's endless questions about Demons. She was waiting for Lana to get there before she explained who and why she was looking for Louis Maxwell.

After hearing that Ryker had killed everyone in the bar and they were Demons she knew she wasn't going to find the bastard inside. No way was she that lucky. Louis was human. A human who used Demons for his own greed. But she had to do a walk through just to make sure. She could have let Charger do it, but he had lied once, and it would take her a while to trust him where this matter was concerned.

"So, you and Charger, huh." Susan said looking everywhere but Raven.

"So, you and Ryker, huh." Raven retorted with a grin.

"Okay fine, I'll mind my own business." Susan rolled her eyes and Raven noticed her gaze went straight to Ryker. "And there is no me and Ryker. He looks at me like a…"

Raven waited really wanting to hear what Susan was about to say. She liked her a lot. She was funny and a few times Raven wondered if she was somehow related to Steve in a second or third cousin way that neither of them realized.

"Bug splattered on his windshield." Susan finished after a long thoughtful pause.

"He just killed a dozen Demons because of you." Raven gave her a sideways glance. "Plus, you are beautiful with that mane of blonde hair, gorgeous round blue eyes and a body that makes men stutter. I seriously don't think Ryker sees you as a bug splattered on his windshield."

"Uh, that's what he does for a living or…whatever." Susan gave her a duh look.

"No, that's what Dark Guardians do for a living." Raven gave her a duh look right back. "Ryker is a VC Warrior who kills vampires and shit, not Demons unless they are in his way. In this case they were threatening you."

"Oh." Susan looked to be deep in thought, remaining silent until she looked at Raven. "So, you really think my eyes are gorgeous?"

Raven frowned glancing at Susan who was batting her eyelashes with outrageous exaggeration that had her bursting out laughing. "You aren't right."

"What's wrong with your eyes?" Charger asked frowning at Susan.

"She thinks I have gorgeous eyes, Charger. You better treat her right or I'm going to steal her away from your ass." Susan warned him then grabbed her phone. "Now where in the hell is Lana. I'm so hungry I could eat a cow. And I have chickens to feed. Beans to pick. A rooster to kill if he got in my beans. Seriously, she thinks I've got all day to wait on her ass."

Raven watched Susan walk away with the phone to her ear. This woman had just faced down a bar full of Demons, got attack by another one and she's worried about her chickens. "She's a mess." Raven shook her head with a chuckle.

"I think she's crazy." Charger said, then snorted. "Scary to say, but she reminds me of a female version of Steve."

"Oh, my God." Raven clapped her hands together. "I thought the same thing. I think that's why I like her so much."

Charger grinned leaning against the car next to her. "You okay?" He asked, changing the subject.

"Yeah, I'm good." Raven shrugged. "Ready to get out of here, but I promised to tell Susan and Lana what's going on. I never really explained to them about Louis. It's only fair that they know if they are going to help me."

"Do you really think that is a good idea." Charger frowned glancing at Susan who was talking animatedly on the phone. "They are human, Raven. We know that even though Louis is human he uses Demons, lots of Demons."

Raven nodded also looking toward Susan. No way in hell did she want anything to happen to her friends. "I'm going to tell them everything but steer them in different safer directions to help me."

"Lana is a good cop." Charger reminded her. "And I hear Susan is just as good. You really think they are going to fall for being led on fake leads."

"I'm still working that out." Raven sighed rubbing her forehead. Then glanced toward the road where Lana and Sid were pulling up on Sid's bike. She looked back at Charger. "I guess I'm going to have to let Sloan know."

"Yeah, about that." Charger frowned nodding back toward where Sid and Lana had just pulled in. Sloan was a few seconds behind them on his own bike and a scowl on his face.

"Damn, how does he know about everything? Is he God or something? Shit!" Raven cursed wishing with everything she had that she was back in her tub soaking away.

Sloan got off his bike and headed straight for her. "How you feeling, Raven?"

"I, ah, huh?" Raven stuttered because honestly, she was expecting a true ass chewing so his question threw her. "Fine."

"Good." Sloan said with a nod, then his whole personality changed. "Now explain to me what the fuck is going on and why I have three dumbasses calling the compound in a panic trying to locate you."

"Um, those would be my three dumbasses." Susan said raising her hand. Sloan looked at her as if he didn't know who the hell she was. "I'm Susan." She said slowly as a reminder. Raven cringed watching Sloan. He was close to losing his shit.

"I know who the hell you are, but that didn't answer my question." Sloan growled his gaze shooting back to Raven. "Is this something the VC should be concerned with or is this a Dark Guardian issue?"

"It's a personal issue." Raven straightened looking him right in the eyes.

"Then it *is* a VC issue." Sloan gave her a nod. "Explain."

Raven looked around to see everyone staring at her. Well here goes nothing she thought just as Jared pulled up. Their eyes locked until she looked away. "Louis Maxwell was and probably still is a major player in the Demon trade." Raven began hating having to retell this story. "Who I thought was dead until I found out differently the night Mayor Groper was murdered. The Guardians had a large sting operation to take him down. Each of our units had different locations to hit. My unit was to hit his primary house. Intel said he wouldn't be there, but at one of his trading locations. We were informed that no one was in residence other than the guards who we quickly took care of."

Memories flooded her mind quickly as that night replayed in her head. She remained silent trying her best to get her emotions in check. Charger was right. After that night it took her a long time to function again.

"We each had a section of house to search. We were looking for anything from information to tell us where innocent people who were to be traded were being held to actually humans being held prisoner inside the residence." Raven cleared her throat. "What I did find was Delilah Maxwell, pregnant and scared to death. She begged me to take her with me. Told me everything I asked, where to find stuff, etc. She was young, terrified, and wanted nothing but to leave Louis."

Raven cursed and pushed away from the car. She paced back and forth reliving it all over again.

"The bastard was watching everything from inside the house. Saw his wife betray him to me." Raven felt herself grinding her teeth in rage. "He was there the whole time, and I never knew it until it was too late. I told her that I would take her with me. I called it in. Back up was coming just in case Louis somehow got word what his wife was doing. Little did we know he already knew. She went upstairs to their bedroom to get a few things. I wasn't worried because we had already cleared the place and I still had a few areas to check. After a while when she didn't come down, I headed up to see what was taking her so long." Raven stopped pacing, then looked directly at Charger. "He had her on their balcony. The bastard was waiting for me to come up. He thanked me for showing him who the real traitor was, his wife. But in the same breath he blamed me for her betraying him, saying that for as long as I live no one close to me would be safe until he was done playing with me and then he would end my life as well. He was unstable, a little manic and a lot crazy. That happens to humans who spend a lot of time in the presence of Demons. He was a powerful man and Demons gravitate toward power."

Looking away from Charger she absently rubbed her chest. She could still feel the pain sometimes from the bullet that went straight through her.

"I knew he was going to push her. I saw it in his eyes. She knew it also because she begged, cried, and pleaded for him not to do it. She said she would kill me herself to prove her loyalty. For a second it looked like he was thinking about it, but I knew better. Men like Louis Maxwell didn't take traitors lightly even if it was his pregnant wife." Raven hissed in anger at the memory. "He told her that he would give her one chance, but he was putting her life in my hands. If I reached her in time, he would let us both live. I knew it was a lie, but the look in her eyes as she stared at me, the person she just promised to kill if he gave her another chance, would haunt me.

"Listen, that's enough for me." Susan said when Raven paused. "The guys a dangerous asshole. End of story. Seriously, Rave, you don't have to say anything else."

Raven looked toward Susan giving her a small smile. "Yeah, I do." She nodded. "I have to because anyone in his path will find out the hard way how crazy and evil he is. He may be human, but his mind and soul is all Demon. Make no mistake about that. Just as he went to push her; I pulled my gun. He already had his pointed at me. Struck me in the chest. Bullet went straight through but didn't stop me. I knew I hit him but wasn't sure where. I ran toward his wife, my hand grabbed hers just in time. Her eyes filled with fear met mine just as everything went black. The next thing I knew I was waking up three days later being told I had failed. Delilah Maxwell had died and the rumor going around was that I had killed her. And in truth I did."

"Bullshit." Lana said shaking her head. "He killed his wife, not you."

Hearing that so many times Raven didn't even respond. "I was lied to and told that Louis Maxwell had been killed by my bullet. It wasn't until I found out the night Mayor Groper was murdered that Louis was still alive. And it wasn't until that night that I knew the bastard was behind the bombing at Tracy and Jake's wedding. Why he has waited this many years, I don't know, but what I do know is I will find the bastard and kill him."

"Not if I get to him first." Jake's voice came from behind her.

"Jake." Raven gasped turning to see Jake staring at her. "I'm so sorry."

Jake walked past everyone and took Raven in his arms. "Nothing for you to be sorry for, Raven. Nothing at all. You've blamed yourself enough for what that bastard did to his wife. I refuse to let you blame yourself for him killing mine."

No one said a word as they processed what they were just told. Only four people present knew that story and what they were up against. Now everyone knew and soon more would know. Raven had tried to prepare herself for that moment, but it was hard. She wasn't like most Guardians or even Warriors. Human deaths haunted her especially if it was by her hand. There were times it had to be done and she did it. It was the innocent humans that haunted her day and night. But now she knew the whole truth. Delilah may not have died that night.

"Jake, they never found her body either." Raven whispered as she looked up at him.

He frowned looking at Charger, then back down at her. "I know."

"You knew?" Raven gasped not understanding then a thought occurred to her. "Did Tracy know?"

"No, she didn't. I never told her. Only myself, Charger, Jared and Kane knew the truth. It was a joint decision not to tell you. Was it the right decision? I don't know now, but at the time it was." Jake said and the relief Raven felt made her weak. It would have devastated her to think Tracy had kept that from her. "Raven even if Delilah Maxwell survived that fall, she didn't live long. None of it was your fault and you have to stop blaming yourself. But if we would have told you the son of bitch was alive you would have gone to the ends of the earth to find the bastard and you were in no shape to do that."

"That was my decision to make." Raven sighed shaking her head. "Not anyone else's."

"I'm not sorry." Jake said without apology. "To keep you safe was our first priority."

Raven looked up at Jake, then to Jared, Kane and then Charger. None of them looked apologetic. They had done what they thought was right for her at the time because they cared. Her throat felt tight as she tried to blink away the tears threatening to fall. Looking back up at Jake, she hugged him.

"I promise you as I've promised Tracy, he will pay for what he's done." Raven whispered, then looked up at him. "I miss her."

"She's missed you also." Jake whispered back softly. "You haven't visited her in a while."

Surprised she looked up at him. "No, I haven't." She said confused, but he only smiled, kissed her on the forehead and then walked away toward Kane.

CHAPTER 18

Charger stood next to Raven as she stood talking to Lana and Susan. They were almost done here, he was just waiting for Kane to finish making sure the woman was okay. He would then take her to a hospital where she could get checked out.

"Charger." Sloan called out nodding him over to where he stood with Jared, Sid and Ryker. Sloan glanced first at Jared and then back to Charger. "Why did you lie to her about this asshole being dead."

"The bullet was silver." Jared was the first to speak. "We didn't think she was going to make it."

"She survived a silver bullet?" Sloan's eyes widened slightly. "How is that possible?"

"Fuck if we know." Jared said, his eyes narrowing. "But she did. It was either because it passed straight through or she's the luckiest vampire to ever be shot with silver. Then again it could be because she's of my blood and I'm a fucking badass."

"I will definitely talk to Slade about that." Sloan mused, then glanced at them both again.

"What how I'm such a badass?" Jared raised both eyebrows. "I can tell you that boss, you don't need Slade for that."

"Shit." Sid laughed shaking his head. "You're fucked up, man."

"Jared, shut the hell up." Sloan growled, then looked at Charger. "Why did you lie to her that they were dead."

"When she did wake up, she remembered everything and took Delilah Maxwell's death hard. She blamed herself. Was reckless with her need for vengeance. It changed her. She has never been the same. If we had told Raven, there was a possibility Delilah lived and in truth she hadn't it would be like her living through it again. We decided not to put her through that." Charger replied glancing back at Raven and realized it was true. She had changed, built walls that he hadn't even been able to crack. Then again had he ever really tried?

"As for Louis, we were hunting for him day and night, but the bastard disappeared. None of us had ever stopped looking, going after leads, but nothing ever turned up. Because of Raven's need for vengeance against the bastard we felt it best to allow her to believe he was dead. Jake is right. She took it hard, she wasn't in the mindset to hunt, let alone be smart when it came to Louis Maxwell at that time." Jared explained, then confessed. "I told her he had died from her bullet. Had a fake death certificate because he was human, for proof. That was all me, my ideal."

"And I went along with it." Charger replied feeling somewhat guilty about his role in the lie. But at the time it was what they had to do. "We have searched for this motherfucker ever since, but it was always dead-end after dead-end. The bastard was ruined after the information his wife gave Raven as well as everything the other units found. He went so far underground that even our best couldn't find him."

"So why do you think he has surfaced now, and do you think he is the one responsible for the explosion at the Guardian wedding?" Sloan asked them both.

"He's back to fulfill the promise he made to Raven." Charger said without hesitation. "He's built his army of Demons again and is feeling confident. And yes, I do believe he was the one responsible for the explosion."

"He's a dangerous man which is why we have been looking for the son of a bitch all this time." Jared said, his joking tone had turned serious.

"Is that why you've been calling off so much?" Sloan asked Jared.

"She's my daughter. If I get a lead, I'm taking it." Jared said without apology.

"I want any information on this fucker you can give me." Sloan told Charger who nodded in agreement. He then looked toward the bar. "No matter how deep this asshole is hiding we will find him. How did Susan come by knowing about this place? Wait, let me guess. Informant."

"You win the prize." Susan said as she followed Raven and Lana into their conversation. "Yes, an informant told me that this Louis asshole is associated with this place. But since Rambo over there killed them all there is no one to question."

"Excellent movie." Jared commented with a grin.

"Thank you!" Susan replied with an exaggerated sigh. "Finally, someone who gets my movie plugs. Anyhoo, I haven't checked the vehicles because I was told to stay, I think it would be worth a shot to see if there is any evidence to be found."

"Good idea." Charger said, then waved over a few Guardians who had just arrived.

"I thought so." Susan said and Charger noticed she gave Ryker a narrowed gaze.

"Can you guys check out these cars, see if there is anything out of the ordinary? Ask Kane for the details." Charger nodded to where Kane was.

"Sure thing." One said as they headed that way.

"Are you by chance related to Steve?" Jared was looking at Susan, his head cocked to the side as if really studying her.

"Took the words right out of my mouth." Sid added staring at Susan.

Charger chuckled as did Raven. "Actually, I wondered the same thing."

"Nope." Susan shook her head. "Loner here. No family. Wait. Isn't he the young funny guy?"

Jared nodded with a grin. "When he's not being annoying, he's funny. Yeah, that's him."

"So, you are calling me funny and annoying?" Susan frowned at Jared. "Annoyingly funny?"

Charger glanced at Jared who was unusually silent. He shifted uncomfortably. "Well, no. I, ah, didn't—"

"I'm just messing with you." She laughed at Jared's uncomfortableness. "I am annoyingly funny. It's all good. But no, as I said loner here. No family. He sounds like a pretty cool dude though."

"Goddamn, she got you good, bro." Sid gave Susan an approving grin.

Charger smiled really liking Susan and he knew Raven felt the same way. She just had an easy going, but in your face personality. Definitely someone you wanted on your side.

"I'll go help them search the cars like I was going to do earlier." Susan started to leave, but Sloan stopped her.

"We no longer need your services." Sloan said causing Susan to stop in her tracks.

"My services." Susan turned to stare at him. "I don't recall offering my services to you."

Sloan didn't back down which wasn't a big shocker. He never backed down. Charger glanced at Raven to see her also frowning at Sloan. This could get ugly real quick.

"This is now VC and Guardian business. We don't need your services nor those of your informants." Sloan said as if to dismiss her. "Because of you one of my Warriors was pulled from his duties."

"I didn't call your Warrior for help." Susan also wasn't backing down.

"Okay, ah, Susan why don't you come with me." Lana tried to interrupt the conversation, but Susan wasn't having it.

Charger glanced at Raven who was still glaring at Sloan. He tried to get her attention, but she was too focused on what was happening with her friend. Sloan was pretty much shitting on Susan's help. If anything, Raven was very loyal, and he knew she was about to stand up for her friend which in turn was going to put her on the bad side of Sloan. Not that he wouldn't mind having her back with the Guardians, but after what she went through today, he knew that isn't where she wanted to be right now.

"You may not have, but your boys did." Sloan replied with a cocked eyebrow.

"My…boys." Susan pulled out of Lana's grasp. "No wait a minute, Lana. My boys? You mean the boys who spent hours working with Jinx to help you break into the police and government systems? Those boys?"

Sloan didn't say anything just continued to stare at Susan as if he had said his final words. Unfortunately, Susan hadn't said hers. But before she could one of the Guardians walked over.

"Found this." He handed it to Charger. Opening the envelope Charger read the handwritten note and cursed. A picture fell out from between two pages and landed face up. Raven's face stared up at him. Bending he picked it up and stared at it. It was Raven walking out of the warehouse. He stared at it then read the note again before reading it out loud.

She stays alive at all cost. Anyone else is fair game. She dies you do not get the rest of your money. Maxwell.

"It has the date, time and address of Tracy and Jake's wedding." Charger informed them then handed Raven the papers and picture when she held out her hand for it.

"You're welcome." Susan said with enough sarcasm that no one could miss it. Charger didn't miss the sadness in her eyes as she turned to walk away. By the look on Ryker's face, he knew he hadn't missed it either.

"She offered me help and I took it." Raven said looking up from the note. "Her and her team as well as Lana. They are damn good at what they do obviously and have informants that we don't have access to." She held up the note proving her point.

"She's human, Raven." Sloan frowned down at her. "We all know what would have happened here if Ryker hadn't shown up."

Charger watched Raven closely. He knew she was struggling with the human factor also, but Raven was Raven and would do what she wanted.

"I'm hiring them on my own. I take full responsibility. They know the risks, even more so now. The VC has no say in what I do outside of the VC as long as it's legal." Raven said, then folded the note sticking it in her pocket along with the picture. "And if you or the Council as a whole has a problem with that then let me go."

"You don't have faith in your own team?" Sloan asked, his voice held no emotion.

"I never said that." Raven also kept her tone level and emotionless. "But I will stop at nothing to find the son of a bitch responsible for my friend's death even if that means having outside help."

She turned to walk away but stopped and faced Sloan again.

"Don't ever question my loyalty again, sir." Raven said, her shoulders straight and head held high. "Next time you do you will not have to worry about letting me go because I will walk without any regrets."

"I never questioned your loyalty, Raven." Sloan corrected her.

"In my world faith in my team and loyalty go hand in hand." Raven answered then turned to walk away.

Many times, Raven had made him proud, but Charger had to say at this very moment he had never been more fucking proud of anyone in his life than he was of her.

"She's a pistol ain't she?" Jared said with a whistle. "Chip off the old block."

"Jesus." Sid walked away shaking his head.

Charger glanced at Sloan to see him turn away, but a smile was spreading across his face as he went toward his bike. Seemed like he wasn't the only one who was proud of Raven. She was one hell of a woman, and it was time he told her that.

CHAPTER 19

Raven headed toward Susan who was getting into her car. The note written by the hand of the man she hated more than anything burned her and yet, she kept it. Not as a reminder, but for the day she finds the son of a bitch and shove it down his throat right before she kills him for real this time. Reliving that night and what followed had her on edge. The dark place she had found herself in was beckoning her, but she refused to be lured there again.

"Susan, wait." Raven called out. Lana jogged up next to her.

Popping back out of her car Susan waited for them. "Sorry if I caused you trouble." Susan frowned at Raven. "He just pissed me off."

"Yeah, Sloan pisses a lot of people off." Raven said, then grinned when Lana agreed with her. Her grin faded as she looked at both women. "Listen, you both are human."

"Great, here we go with the human shit again." Susan rolled her eyes glancing at Lana. "How many times have we heard that?"

"More times that I can count." Lana said with a frown.

"Seriously when did it become a crime to be human?" Susan threw her hands up in the air. "I actually like it. Has its perks, maybe not like you know, immortality, but we don't need to drink blood. Yuck. We get to sleep which is my most favorite hobby ever. Especially on rainy days."

Raven sighed listening to Susan's long list of why being human rocked. "Does she always talk this much?"

Lana laughed with a nod. "Wait until you're around her when she's nervous." Lana snorted. "Nonstop doesn't even describe it."

"I mean seriously what's so cool about being immortal other than, you know, being immortal?" Susan finally stopped her list to ask that question. "Well, and looking young forever, but damn who wants to live forever. People piss me off too much to live that damn long. I'd probably turn bad and just start killing assholes."

"We can have sex nonstop for days." Raven threw that out there wanting to mess with Susan just to see her reaction, but honestly it was a true fact.

Susan opened her mouth, shut it, and stared at Raven for a long minute before opening her mouth again with a half grin. "You're fucking with me." Susan said, then her mouth opened wide when Raven shook her head. "Even guys? No way. They don't roll over and go right to sleep. Oh, wait. Vampires don't sleep. So, you are telling me that they don't need recovery time?"

"Nope, no recovery time." Raven shook her head loving the look on Susan's amazed face.

"Holy shit." Susan said staring off thinking about that little bit of information. She then looked at Lana with wide eyes. "You poor thing....or you very lucky lady."

"It's nice." Lana grinned nodding her head. "Really nice."

Susan's amazement suddenly turned into a crest fallen expression.

"What's wrong?" Raven asked glancing at Lana then back to Susan.

"I really wish you wouldn't have told me that." Susan said with a huge sigh. "Single with no immortal prospects." She pointed to herself.

Glancing toward Ryker who glanced their way Raven grinned. "Oh, I don't know about that. I'm sure Ryker would be more than happy to go a few nonstop rounds with you."

"Bug. Windshield. Splatter. Remember?" Susan snorted rolling her eyes. "Plus, I'd have to have someone who isn't afraid of spiders."

"What?" Both Raven and Lana frowned confused.

"Yeah, all that's down here is cobwebs and shit." Susan motioned toward her privates. "Ain't seen action in a looong time."

Not much shocked or surprised Raven, but Susan seemed to do just that all the damn time. Laughter filled her soul as she bent over laughing so hard she thought she was going to puke. Lana was having the same problem.

"Wow, didn't know my nonexistent sex life was so damn funny." Susan grumbled, but Raven saw a small smile slip across her face and knew that Susan was doing her best to help Raven forget the memories she had just shared with them all. For that she owed this woman a lot because it meant everything to her that someone cared so much.

"Sorry." Raven choked out. "Just didn't expect you to say that."

"Eh, it's all good." Susan shrugged. "Listen, Rave. I'm here and not going anywhere. I don't care what the Mr. Grand VC Master Sloan guy over there says. He doesn't control me. Not my boss and definitely don't pay me shit. I will continue hunting this asshole. I'm not stupid as the five Stooges over there think I am. I'm getting silver bullets infused with Holy water ASAP. And I will do my best not to go out on my own, but no promises on that since you both suck at answering your phones."

"It's the three Stooges." Lana corrected her still chuckling at Susan.

Susan looked toward the men, then counted using her finger. "Nope." She shook her head. "It's five."

Raven glanced that way to see them all looking at them. Charger, Ryker, Jared and Sid headed their way. "Hey, Ryker." Raven said as they approached. "You scared of spiders?"

Ryker frowned giving Raven a suspicious look. "No." His answer was spoken as if it was a trick question and in a way it was.

Raven cocked her eyebrow, her grin hurting her still bruised cheeks as she gave Susan a sideways glance. "Interesting."

"Bug. Windshield. Splatter. But good try friend." Susan winked at her then turned to get into her car after giving Lana a quick hug. "I would hug you, Raven, but you look a little sore. I'll get ya next time. Ryker thanks for being my Rambo. You seriously have to watch this movie. Okay, peeps. It's been a fun learning experience on Demons and creepy wall climbers, but I've got to run. I got cucumbers coming in and a Rooster to feed. Need to take care of both since old Drumstick is the only cock I've seen in quite a while. Later."

Everyone was silent, well except for Raven and Lana who were laughing at Susan's sexual innuendo. Raven couldn't even express the gratitude she felt for Susan at this very moment. She had just revealed such a darkness from her past that would normally set her back, but Susan made sure that didn't happen without really knowing what she was doing…or did she.

"What is it with you women and the word cock." Jared grumbled looking at both Lana and Raven.

"I like cucumbers." Sid announced then jumped when both Raven and Lana screamed with laughter. "What in the hell is wrong with you two? Charger how do you know if someone is possessed? I think these two need to get checked out."

"Damn." Raven chuckled trying to calm down. "My rib is hurting again."

"You're just now starting to really get to know her. Just wait." Lana said, clearing the laughter from her throat. "I've dealt with this for years and it just keeps going and going."

"I'm looking forward to it." Raven said finally able to talk normal. She glanced at Ryker who was watching Susan's car disappear up the dirt drive. His gaze shifted to hers. Raven just raised both eyebrows as if to say, yeah, she's into you dumbass. Not knowing if he took her subtle message or not, she sighed.

"So, you're not listening to Sloan." Jared cocked his eyebrow at her. "She's human, Raven. We are dealing with Demons. I don't think this is going to end well."

"Do you feel the same way?" Lana asked Sid putting both hands on her hips. "Because as you all may have forgotten I am working with Susan again and oh, look, I'm human also."

"Why do I feel like this is a no win for me question?" Sid sighed rubbing his forehead. "Lana this is a whole different beast. I have to say I'm with Sloan on this one."

"Of course, you are." Lana glared at him. "Same old song and dance. You're female. You're human. You're a human female. Did you know that Susan has found over a thousand missing women and children? Didn't think so. Did you know that she is the best in the field for tracking missing people? Of course not because you never thought to ask."

Raven remained silent listening. Honestly, she didn't know any of this either. Very impressive resume for sure.

"Susan, myself and the team know what the fuck we are doing and have been doing it since before I met any of you." Lana kept on going. "When I first met you and the Warriors you had no clue who we were, Sid. So, stop with this human shit because seriously, don't you think we know we are human and let us do our damn job. I don't know about you guys, but Susan is the first person to actually give Raven a clue about this Maxwell guy. I'd say that deserves some respect and not the typical Warrior response of...*you're human...you're female* bullshit. And yes, Sloan, this is directed at you also."

"I can't be responsible for what happens to humans who think they can do our jobs." Sloan countered still not backing down.

"When did we ever ask for you to take responsibility? Never." Lana said, then glanced at Raven. "And we aren't asking you either. We are doing this, no question about it. It's our main focus and we will find this bastard no matter what it takes."

More than anyone standing there Raven got it. She understood exactly what Lana was saying. Being a woman in a man's world sucked. She could only imagine what it was like to be a human woman in an immortal man's world. Even though the risks they were taking for her were at the front of her mind, she would make damn sure they stayed safe.

"Do we get vacation time?" Raven asked Sloan before she glanced his way.

"Vacation time." Jared snorted. "What the fuck is that?"

Raven ignored Jared still staring at Sloan. If this was going to happen, she needed to focus on this and this alone, plus she could make sure that Susan and Lana stayed safe. She believed if they worked together and with Susan's skill of finding missing people they could find Louis.

"I need time to heal." Raven added when Sloan continued to glare at her. His eyes shifted toward Lana then back to her. He knew exactly what she was doing.

"You have one week." Sloan's eyes narrowed to slits. "Not a day more."

"What in the actual fuck." Jared straightened with a growl. "I've never had a fucking vacation and my daughter just waltzes in and gets a week. If this is paid, I'm going to lose my shit."

"Thanks, dad, for the concern." Raven rolled her eyes.

Jared snorted looking her up and down. "To heal my ass."

"Raven." Sloan caught her attention. He looked at Lana, then back to her. "Keep me informed…on your healing."

Nodding Raven glanced at Lana giving her a sly wink. Once everyone walked away except for Lana, Sid, and Charger she smiled. "Let Susan know I'll meet you guys first thing in the morning."

"Done." Lana also grinned, but the grin slipped away as she walked past Sid. "You owe me a nice dinner, bud."

Sid watched her walk toward the bike, then turned toward Raven. "I'm trusting you to keep her safe."

"I would lay down my life for her." Raven replied in a true Warrior fashion.

After a few seconds of staring at Raven he nodded. "Guess I need to go make-up with my woman. I have a feeling this is going to be a very expensive dinner."

"So, you have nothing to say?" Raven asked Charger who had remained oddly silent throughout most of the conversations.

"No." Charger pushed away from the car he was leaning against. He took her hand leading her to the car.

He opened the door for her, she started to get in but stopped, turning her head she looked up at him. "Who are you?" She said in a teasing manner, but honestly, she was really wanting to know.

Charger gave her the most charming smile she had ever seen. She felt it to her toes. "The man who believes in you, Raven."

Giving him a smile of her own she turned and mouthed the word 'wow' as she climbed into the SUV. She never realized before how much those words coming from his mouth would mean to her. And if he was trying to get her to admit she wanted sex with him…well, he was definitely on the right track. He shut her door then walked around glancing at her from the front of the SUV giving her a wink. "Lord have mercy." She whispered feeling every nerve ending in her body spring to life.

CHAPTER 20

After getting home Susan showered and changed, she made herself a quick sandwich. Sitting down at her tiny table she started to eat, but it felt like sandpaper in her mouth. She really didn't have an appetite. She put up a brave face in front of others, but in truth she was lonely. She hated eating alone. She used to have dinner with her father when she wasn't working, but now that he was gone it was just her. Damn, she missed him.

Aggravated at feeling sorry for herself, Susan jumped up grabbing her plate. Placing it and her sandwich that had one bite out of it in the sink she sighed looking out the window. Deciding to do some garden work she slipped on her tennis shoes, grabbed her garden basket, and headed out to her place of escape.

Eyeing Drumstick who was pecking around the area she hurried past him. He seemed preoccupied which was fine with her. She wasn't in the mood to go a round or two with him. Damn bird kept getting out of the pen and she couldn't figure out how. The sneaky fucker. Every single time she thought she figured it out he'd escape again.

Heading toward the beans she glanced at the cabbage and stopped dead. Something had been eating her cabbage. Her head snapped toward Drumstick knowing exactly who the culprit was. "Damn it, Drumstick." She growled at the rooster. "What did I tell you about the garden? Hmmm? Off limits you sack of feathers. I swear I'm going to wring that neck of yours one day and fry you up."

He still ignored her as if he didn't have a care in the world. Lucky fucker. Making her way down one row of beans she knelt where she had left off. One day she would learn to can her vegetables, but for right now she'd eat them, give them to her team or elderly neighbors.

As she worked, she let her mind wander as she usually did. Most of the time it was about work and what she needed to accomplish or who she needed to find, informants she needed to contact and so on. Tonight, it was different. Tonight, a certain Warrior was on her mind. Susan sighed as she tossed a hand of green beans into the basket. The way he had looked when he burst through the bar door today, the relief she had felt at seeing him and how he didn't show any fear at all made her shiver.

"Just stop." She hissed to herself. "Bug splatter is all you are and will ever be to a man like him, Susan Marie." She used her middle name whenever she was giving herself shit.

Swiping a stray hair out of her face she frowned. Usually, she wasn't attracted to overbearing men, but Ryker was different. Even when he was being harsh with her all she could think about was what he would look like without a shirt on. Susan snorted shaking her head as she continued to pick beans now with a vengeance. Usually, she was gentle because there were still tiny beans and blooms on the plants, but that all went out the window as she thought about Ryker's bare torso.

"You're an idiot, Susan Marie." She said as she continued to pick and toss, pick and toss. "You're a foul mouth, in your face, think you're funny kind of girl. What man wants that. Certainly not a man like him."

Hearing a noise, she cursed without looking up. "I'm not in the mood Drumstick." Susan warned him. "You better not peck me you little pecker head."

A boot appeared in the row in front of her, she discreetly grabbed the garden scissors next to her knee. Her eyes scanned up a muscular leg, past a nice jean clad bulge to a black skin tight t-shirt and finally to a familiar face. Ryker stared down at her, his golden eyes going from hers to the scissors in her tight grip.

"Nice move." He commented, then grinned. "Were you going to stab me in the knee?"

It was her eyes that moved this time, but downward then back up again. "A little higher."

His grin widened. "That would have worked better than the knee."

"I thought you were Drumstick coming in for a sneak attack." Susan said putting the scissor back down. "What are you doing here?"

"Drumstick is back with his ladies." Ryker nodded his head in that direction. "I put him back in the pen while you were talking to yourself, Susan Marie."

Susan felt her face flame wondering how much he heard of the conversation she was having with herself. Holy shit, if he heard one word of what she said she was going to throw herself in the pen with Drumstick so he could peck her to death.

"Susan Marie is what I call myself when I'm telling myself off." Susan shrugged then grabbed a handful of beans off the vine because honestly, she didn't know what else to do. She was definitely unprepared to see him standing in the middle of her garden with her face directly across from his well-endowed crotch. Oh, the dreams she will have about this moment. She snorted to herself. "I talk to myself often. My shrink says it's perfectly normal as long as I don't answer myself back."

Ryker actually laughed at that, then stared down at her. "That is a beautiful name."

"Thank you. Marie was my mother's first name. My dad called me Susan Marie whenever I was in trouble which was quite often. Shocker, huh." Susan felt herself blush again. What in the hell was wrong with her? She blushed more in the past minute than she had in her entire life. She needed to play it cool and stop talking so damn much. "Seriously, what are you doing here? To remind me I'm not a cop anymore? I'm sorry, that was rude."

"I deserved that." Ryker gave her nod.

"No, you didn't." Susan sighed looking down at her plants. "I'm like a Pitbull, sometimes I can't seem to let things go. Another social glitch in a long list of social glitches I have going for me."

"You are not a Pitbull nor are you bug splatter." Ryker's deep voice radiated over her sending heat to every single part of her body. She then realized what he just said.

"You heard that?" Susan groaned then grabbed the scissor and raised them toward him. He took them from her.

"What am I doing with these?" Ryker asked sounding a little confused.

Keeping her head down in total embarrassment she pointed to her heart. "Kill me now." She begged him dramatically. "Make it fast, but please kill me."

Kneeling he put the scissors in the basket. "Any man who doesn't see a beautiful, intelligent, hilariously funny woman who could put anybody in their place with her colorful language doesn't deserve someone like…Susan Marie."

"Wow." She mouthed the word still staring at her lap afraid if she looked up, she would leap into his big muscular arms making a bigger fool of herself. She really wanted to pinch her arm to make sure Drumstick hadn't done a sneak attack sending her into unconsciousness and she wasn't really lying in her beans knocked out having this amazing dream.

"And I'm sorry for being so harsh on you today." Ryker touched her chin lifting her face up to his. "I'm very protective and when I saw you surrounded by Demons it just set me off. I shouldn't have taken it out on you like that."

"No need to apologize." She replied with a shrug a little shocked. "My dad always told me I was a lot for such a small package. Most could only take me in small doses and to ignore the ones who couldn't."

"Your father sounds like he was a good man." Ryker said with a softness in his voice she had never heard from him before. Not that she knew him all that well.

"He was the best." Susan smiled with a daughter's pride. "When I wasn't working, I had dinner with him every night. We both hated to eat alone. He was a good listener, and I was a good talker. He truly believed in what I did for people and was my biggest supporter. His love for action movies rubbed off on me. Rambo was his favorite movie. He would have really liked you." She snorted giving him a half grin.

Ryker stayed silent as she went on about her dad, but she couldn't seem to stop. Since his death she hadn't had any one to talk to about how awesome he was except for Drumstick who had more brains in his ass than his head.

"Sorry." Susan gave a half laugh. "Don't know why all that came out of my mouth like word vomit. I'm sure you have better things to do than listen to me go on and on."

"You miss him. It's normal for you to want to talk about him. There is nothing wrong with that. I'm sorry I never got to meet him." Ryker said and sounded like he meant it.

"Yeah, he was one of the good ones." Susan said blinking back tears. "I could always be myself with him."

"As you should always be." He replied searching her eyes. "You're a very special person, Susan. Never forget that."

Susan frowned pulling herself out of what seemed like a romance book moment wondering if she was being played. No man in her history of men had ever said all the right things and Ryker was hitting them out of the park. Every single word had her drooling, panting, and wanting like she had never drooled, panted, or wanted before in her life. She warned herself once again to play it cool, guard her stupid ass heart and not be that girl who gets played by the sexy, very muscular, long-haired Warrior with eyes the color of gold that seemed to see inside her soul. Holy shit she was fucked.

"Speaking of Rambo. Someone told me I needed to see this movie." Ryker stood pulling out the DVD package. "Thought maybe I could find someone to watch it with me."

Shocked to the core Susan's mouth opened wide staring at the cover of Rambo. She jumped up almost falling into her beans. He grasped her arm to steady her. "Yes!" She said excitedly. So much for playing it cool. "Sorry, obviously I don't get much company." She rolled her eyes at herself.

"Then I'm honored to invite myself to be you company if that's okay with you." Ryker grinned as she headed toward the house.

"Hells yeah, it's okay with me. The less time I spend with myself the better." She said, then frowned. "Oh, wait I have to close the chickens in. Been hearing a lot of coyotes lately. If anything happened to my girls, I'd be a mess."

"What about old Drumstick?" Ryker teased helping her close them in for the night. "He on his own with the coyotes?"

"As much as he pisses me off, I can't leave him to fend for himself." Susan said shooing him inside the chicken house. He flapped his wings at her after doing his little 'I'm going to spur you dance' but went inside with the others without too much fuss. "He's a pain in my ass, but he's grown on me."

After making sure everything was locked up tight, they headed into the house with Susan wondering how in the hell this was even happening. She had started the night alone, having a moment of feeling sorry for herself and now this handsome Warrior was inside her house ready to sit on her couch and watch one of her favorite movies. Why? That question kept coming into her mind and she really kind of wanted to know. Doubts flooded her head and she tried to push them away. Why couldn't she just take things and go with them instead of over analyzing it to death? Because that's not who she was, that's why.

"Susan?" Ryker noticed her sudden change.

Susan sighed turning toward him. "Are you here because you feel sorry for me?"

"What?" Ryker frowned and genuinely looked confused by her question.

"Listen I know this is strange and well, I'm a lot strange but just go with it okay?" Susan said without hesitation. "I promise you I won't freak out or anything, but are you here because you feel sorry for me?"

"I went into a store I've never been to before to get a movie I had to have someone search for when I could have gone to have a nice dinner, go to my place and relax." Ryker replied, his eyes never leaving hers. "I would not do that for someone I felt sorry for. I would however do that for someone I'd like to spend time with instead of sitting alone at my place. So, the answer to your questions is no, sorry is definitely not what I feel for you."

They stood in her small kitchen staring at each other for a long time. Susan believed him. She wanted to scream, 'good answer' but refrained. Instead, she asked him the next most important question. "So, are you a chip or popcorn guy?" She smiled brightly at him.

"Definitely popcorn." Ryker chuckled shaking his head.

"Good answer." She nodded, then reached for the popcorn feeling happier than she had in a long time, but guarded as she had learned the hard way to be.

CHAPTER 21

Raven stared at the scenery as it passed. After leaving the bar they had stopped for a bite to eat. Her face was still bruised, but the swelling was almost gone. That didn't stop people from staring and then glaring at Charger. The waitress was downright rude to him, but as sweet as she could be to Raven. Even slipped her a note asking if she needed help. A grin slipped across her lips as she glanced at Charger. The dashboard lights lit his handsome face. He looked over at her.

"What are you grinning about?" He asked before looking back at the road.

"How all the women in the restaurant were wanting to kill you." Raven replied with a chuckle.

Charger made a noise in the back of his throat. "Glad you find it amusing. I, on the other hand, don't like to be labeled as an abuser."

"It's not every day I get to see you uncomfortable. But you're right and I did tell the waitress that I was in a car accident and that you were a very good man. Word got around the restaurant and the glares stopped. I think if I would have told them the truth Sloan would have a whole lot of women on his doorstep demanding answers." Raven said, then frowned. "Damn, that would have been a good payback."

"You definitely like living dangerously don't you." Charger laughed loudly as he pulled up to her place.

"Yeah, well he can be an asshole sometimes." Raven replied as they stopped in front of her place. She had tried living in an apartment but living so close to strangers didn't suit her very well. Pam had helped her find this small house and she absolutely loved it. It was the first place she had ever owned.

Before she could open her door, Charger was there opening it for her. Sliding out she looked up at him. "Why are you doing this?" Raven frowned up at him. She was tall for a woman, but Charger towered over her.

"Because you deserve it." Charger replied staring down at her.

"But I don't expect it." Raven said, not comfortable playing the woman role. No one had ever opened her car door for her or any door for that matter because she was female. If they tried, she probably would have cussed them out or punched them in the nuts. And yet, it was kind of nice, made her feel special. She also didn't want him doing it because he thought that was what she wanted. What she wanted was much more complicated.

"Yeah, well get used to it." He moved her out of the way so he could shut the door. He pulled her key out of his pocket, reached around her and unlocked the door pushing it open then handed her the key. "Don't leave that outside again. Get a keychain."

Rolling her eyes, she walked inside but stopped and turned. Charger stood outside staring at her. "Aren't you coming in?"

He shook his head. "Not tonight."

A wave of disappointment swarmed her. Her eyes scanned his body as she looked away. Damn, she was hoping…she stopped that thought instantly. "Oh, okay." She nodded not really knowing what else to say. She wasn't sure if she liked this new Charger or not. The saying, careful what you wish for, came to mind. The old Charger would have already been all over her, but that was before. This was now. "Well, ah, thanks for dinner."

"You're welcome, Raven." He said, then winked at her as he closed the door.

She just stared at the closed door with a frown. The fucker knew what his winks did to her. Okay, maybe he didn't know that, but still. Why fucking wink at her all sexy like. Was he playing with her? Did he know she would fall on her knees and do anything he wanted sexually because she was strung so tight in need for him that she could scream?

Fine let him play his games she thought with a growl. She could play to…with herself and take care of her own needs. A vision of Charger on top of her pounding away played through her mind. Yeah, not the same at all.

"Shit!" She cursed as she stomped toward the door and almost pulled it off the hinges. Her poor door was going through hell lately. Charger was backing out of her driveway. Jumping the steps, she bent down grabbing a rock and threw it through the windshield. Oops, maybe she should have yelled, but Raven never did the easier things.

The truck stopped and Charger jumped out of the SUV. "What the hell?" He looked first at her then at the cracked windshield. "You broke the windshield?"

"So." Oh, good comeback Raven, she cursed at herself. "That's what insurance is for?"

"What? Crazy women who throw rocks through a windshield?" Charger threw his hands out to his side. "What is wrong with you?"

"You!" She pointed at him. "You are what's wrong with me."

"What in the hell did I do now?" Charger dropped his arms looking totally confused. "I've done everything I can to treat you how you deserve to be treated."

"I've never asked you to do any of those things, Charger." This time Raven threw her arms out. "I don't need you to open my doors, take me to dinners, pull out my fucking chair, send me flowers though I do like daisies FYI. But I don't need any of that. I just need you to care…about me."

"I have always cared about you. That's what I'm trying to do, dammit." Charger looked and sounded so frustrated Raven felt sorry for him. She knew she could be confusing and a little difficult.

"I want the old you back." Raven said, knowing a point-blank approach was needed.

"The old me?" Charger frowned, his eyes narrowed.

"Yes, the old you, but not the old you that pushed me away." Raven took a step toward him and stopped. "Not the old you that acted like you didn't care for me. Just be the old you, that wants me in his life."

Charger continued to stare at her as he reached in and turned off the SUV then slammed the door closed. Raven took another step close enough that they could touch, but didn't.

"I don't need all that fancy stuff that comes with a relationship, Charger. I never did." Raven sighed hoping he understood what she was desperately trying to stay.

"What if I like doing that...fancy stuff for you?" He tilted his head, a half grin on his face.

"Then do it, but not because you think that's what I want because it's not." Raven answered as honestly as she could.

"What *do* you want, Raven?" Charger asked, his eyes searching hers. "And do not lie to me."

"You." She whispered. "I want you. That's all I've ever wanted."

"You've always had me." Charger replied as he reached out and grabbed her. Wrapping his arms around her waist, Raven gripped him around the neck and climbed up his body to where she straddled him.

Their lips smashed together full of need. Charger's hand tangled in her hair as he tried to pull her mouth closer to his. Raven couldn't get enough of him. It had been so long, at least for her, it had been way too long since she had been held by him. She moaned when he pulled away from her.

"When you say you want me." Charger's words came out a little choppy and rough then he kissed her before pulling away again making her moan louder in frustration. "Are you saying you want me as in…"

"Charger, shut up." Raven pulled his face to hers then whispered against his lips. "I want you inside me…now."

"Fuck!" Charger growled as he rushed toward her door taking the steps two at a time, their mouths still fused together. He slammed the door behind them as he pushed her up against the wall. Raven slipped her legs from around him and slid down his body. Quickly they ripped each other's clothes off each other in their haste. Charger's hands were all over her, rough just like she wanted it. Always wanted it. Charger was a very dominant lover, who took control without asking and even though she was an alpha female she allowed it without question. She wanted a man in her bed, and Charger was all man.

"Are you still sore anywhere?" Charger asked as his fangs raked her neck. She groaned when three of his fingers slipped inside her, then he gave her a quick bite into her skin. "Are you fucking sore anywhere, Raven? Answer me! Fuck, you are so goddamn wet." He pumped his fingers in and out of her while his thumb rubbed against her clit.

The harshness of his words turned her on more. It just showed her how much he wanted her. "No and I swear if you are gentle with me, I will kill you when we're done." She had grabbed his wrist trying to control the tempo he had set with his fingers, and she knew he wasn't going to put up with it… that's why she did it.

"Let go of my wrist." He ordered as he bent taking her nipple into his mouth. He bit, sucked, and licked before lifting her up pulling her away from the wall so he could slap her ass hard. "I said let go of my wrist."

Raven moaned in pure pleasure and did as she was told, instead of his wrist she cupped his balls giving them a squeeze before gripping his cock. She began pumping him in the same rhythm he had set. "Better?" She whispered with a sexy grin, licking one of his nipples.

He began moving his hips as she was moving hers. His groans of pleasure mixed with hers was enough to make her explode but she held back. Looking down at his cock she wanted nothing more than to taste him. Pulling her hand away, she pushed his wrist, so his fingers slipped out of her. Before he could say anything, she was on her knees, her back against the wall as she took him in her mouth.

"Son of a bitch!" He howled as she took him all the way down her throat. He was big, but she had no gag reflex and was very talented in this aspect. Charger put one hand behind her head as he carefully began pumping into her mouth. Their eyes met, she looked up and he looked down as she allowed him to use her mouth. Watching him watch his cock slide in-between her lips was such a turn on for her. Most women she had talked about sex with hated this, but not Raven. She enjoyed it almost as much as the man did. Most men would call Charger a lucky bastard. Charger gave two fast pumps before he gently pulled out of her mouth. "My turn."

His words set her on fire because as good as she was at taking him in her mouth, Charger was an expert with his tongue. He helped her up, his mouth smashed down on hers and she knew he could taste himself which had her pussy clenching like crazy. Charger was open about sex, loved sex and wanted a lot of it…most women would call her a lucky bitch.

Bending Charger hooked his arms under her legs and with her back against the wall he stood up slowly. His breath was warm against her, teasing her to the point she wanted to grab his head and smash his mouth against her, but she refrained. The first lick of his tongue almost sent her flying off his shoulders, it felt so good. As he continued his teasing, she begged him to stop driving her insane.

"Dammit, Charger. I can't take much more." She cried out and she actually felt his smile against her pussy. That's when he ravished her with his mouth and tongue. Without realizing she was doing it, her fingers gripped his hair pulling him into her. He was relentless in his assault, and she loved every single fucking minute of it. Her head fell back against the wall going back and forth, as she cried out in pleasure.

She knew she was close, and so did he because he stopped suddenly, then lowered her to the ground. Picking her up he went to her bed, turned her, pulling her ass up toward him and entered her from behind. One hand was on her hip and the other ran along her side until he cupped and squeezed her breast with just enough pressure to cause a little pain. She moaned as she met him thrust for thrust.

Suddenly he stopped, slipped out of her turning her over where he slid into her again. She grabbed his neck pulling herself up so she could ride him, and ride him she fucking did. Their mouths met in a hungry battle of tongues.

He pulled away as he slowed her down by holding onto her hips. She started to protest, but the look in his eyes stopped her. "You are mine, Raven." Charger said, his eyes searching hers. "You are my Mate."

"As you are mine." Raven said the words as her body tingled all over. "Take my blood."

"As you will take mine." Charger responded as he used her hips moving them slowly on his cock.

"And together we will be one." She whispered, her voice cracking with emotion.

"For all of eternity." He whispered back, his fangs had grown below his upper lip.

"For all of eternity." She repeated his words softly.

She couldn't believe that they had just spoken the Guardian mating ritual, but until they took of each others blood it wasn't a done deal. Slowly she tilted her head, her eyes never leaving his. "Are you sure?" She whispered so softly she wondered if she even said the words out loud. She had wanted this for so long she was terrified she had imagined it.

"Never more sure of anything in my life." He answered tilting his head the opposite way.

Slowly they lowered their mouths and as one they bit into each other's veins. The feelings that overwhelmed Raven was off the charts. Her body was on fire and her need for Charger at that very moment was like nothing she had ever felt. They continued to take each other's blood as Charger began to lift her hips and slam her down on his hard cock. She felt out of control as if she couldn't get enough. Feeling his fangs slip out of her neck, Raven followed suit.

Charger roared as he shifted them so he could pound himself inside of her. Raven moaned and screamed in frustration when she felt like she couldn't get enough. God, this was crazy. Using all the strength she had and taking Charger by surprise she flipped them over, so she was now the one on top. She slammed herself down on him repeatedly. Looking at Charger she saw his eyes were on her bouncing tits as she placed both hands on her thighs to help keep her upright as she lost control.

"Charger!" She cried out a little afraid of the intenseness she was feeling. If felt as if she didn't cum soon, she was going to explode or go insane or both.

"I got you." Charger flipped them again, lifted one of her legs over his shoulder and continued the same rhythm. His fingers found her clit. "You ready." He smiled down at her then played with her clit before giving it a hard pinch. She never had time to answer.

The scream that escaped her mouth surprised even her. Charger roared his own pleasure a few seconds later as he gave one last hard thrust into her body; his head was thrown back as veins popped out on his neck. Raven had never seen anything sexier in her entire life. Her over worked pussy tightened against his cock asking for more.

Charger stared down at her, his arms propping his weight off of her. "Dammit, I wanted to do the mating ritual while making love to you." He said actually looking upset. "But it just happened." His eyes shifted from hers.

Frowning Raven lifted her hand and forced him to look back at her. "Charger. Fucking is making love…to us." She smiled when a grin tipped the corner of his mouth. "Making love is boring. I want to be fucked. What just happened was perfect."

"I love you." Charger vowed. "And I promise that I will never push you aside again. We are going to fight, we are going to disagree, and we are definitely going to piss each other off, but I will come home every single night to make up with you."

A tear slipped from her eye, she felt it roll into her hair as she looked up at him. "That's all I've ever wanted, Charger. And I love you more than you will ever know."

Charger leaned down kissing her softly. Lifting his lips slightly he grinned down at her. "So, you want to…fuck again."

"As long as you're not going to get all girly on me wanting to get soft and make love." Raven teased earning her a slap on the ass when he picked her up off the bed suddenly.

The rest of the night was nothing but bliss. They fucked, laughed, talked, and Raven had never been happier to have the old Charger back. Only once did uncertain fear creep into her soul, but she pushed it back. Everything was going to work out, she had to believe that. Her world was almost perfect, something she never thought would happen and she would die to protect her world.

CHAPTER 22

The credits were rolling on the movie as Ryker and Susan sat on the couch. A big empty bowl that contained popcorn sat between them. Three empty beer bottles sat on the coffee table.

"Okay, so what's your thoughts?" Susan turned toward him pulling her bended legs up hugging them with her arms as her chin rested on her knees. "Inquiring minds want to know."

Ryker grinned as he looked from the television and glanced her way. "Not bad."

"Not bad?" Susan frowned lifting her chin off her knees. "What's that mean...not bad?"

Laughing Ryker stood and stretched. "He could have done some things differently."

"Oh, really." Susan also stood. "Like what?"

"First of all, he pretty much let everyone know what he was going to do." Ryker shrugged. "Not a smart move."

Susan thought about that a minute. "Yeah, okay I see your point. What else?"

"It was a good movie, Susan." Ryker said chuckling. "I'm not going to give a review."

"Well, you're no fun." Susan wrinkled her nose at him with a huff grabbing the few left-over pieces of popcorn and threw them at him. His smile slipped as he continued to stare at her, his golden eyes intent. He moved toward her but stopped.

Susan held her breath praying he was going to kiss her. Not that a Rambo movie caused uncontrollable passion, but hey, a girl could hope.

"I better be going. It's getting late." Ryker said and Susan had to hold back a moan of disappointment.

"Oh, okay." Susan said bending to pick up the popcorn she just threw at him. Geez, why couldn't she be more mature. Once good men really got to know her real personality they ran for the hills.

Grabbing the bowl, she went into the kitchen tossing the kernels into the trash and then tossed it in the sink with her uneaten sandwich.

"You didn't eat your dinner?" Ryker was also looking at her one bite sandwich with a frown.

"Not much for eating alone." She shrugged then smiled. "Plus, I had more room for popcorn. That's always a good thing."

Ryker frowned as he walked to the door, and out onto the back porch. Susan never used her front door. It stuck all the time and she just never got it fixed. She preferred coming in through the back anyway. She followed him out. He stepped down one step then turned around to face her.

"Have dinner with me tomorrow night." Ryker said, his golden eyes glowed in the shadows of the dim porchlight. "I get off shift about seven and can pick you up."

"I would really like that." Susan smiled feeling a blush of pleasure bloom across her face. Maybe she hadn't scared him off like she had thought. "I'll try to behave more mature in public." She teased, but he didn't smile. Instead, he stepped back up on the porch and tilted her face up to his.

"Never change, Susan Marie." His voice was low and deep. Slowly he lowered his head and gently kissed her on the lips before pulling away. "For anyone."

With that he turned away and headed down the steps. The soulful howl of coyotes filled the silence. Ryker stopped looking up at her and she swore her legs were going to give out. The protectiveness that radiated off him was off the charts.

"I'm not leaving until you are safe inside and I hear the door lock." He informed her as he looked up at her.

"Hmm, then maybe I'll just stay right here." She said, then grinned when he cocked his eyebrow at her, but a smile tipped the corner of his nice lips. "Sorry. Okay. Going in and locking up. Goodnight, Ryker."

"Goodnight." He replied as she shut the door and locked it. She leaned against it sliding down to the floor with her hand on her pounding heart. Holy shit she better not have a heart attack before that dinner tomorrow night. She will be so pissed if she missed this date because she died.

Her mind played that kiss over and over again. She didn't know how long she sat on the floor, but when her phone rang, she almost jumped out of her skin. "Shit!" She grabbed her chest again. "Can't I even have a fantasy moment without someone calling me? Guess I can see why no one answers their phone anymore. It's a pain in the ass." She mumbled to herself angry her fantasy daydreaming was being put on hold.

Standing up she rushed over to the table and grabbed it. Griffin's face flashed on the screen.

"Hello. I'm fine, glad you finally called to ask." Susan said walking into the living room to pick up the empty beer bottles. Grabbing Ryker's, she thought about running her tongue over it then snorted at the thought. That man was causing her to lose her damn mind.

"I know you're fine because we watched the whole fucking thing." Griffin said, his voice sounding a little panicked.

"What?" Susan frowned tossing the bottles in the trash, and yes, without licking the rim of Ryker's.

"The VC sent Jinx over to the bar to hack into the computer system there. We went with him. You were already gone, so fuck you, we were there to see if you were okay." Griffin huffed. "The place had hidden cameras everywhere, even in the parking lot. Sam spotted one outside, but once we started to look, they were fucking everywhere. Once he had everything pulled, we went back to the VC and managed to get everything off the cameras as well as broke into the systems that downloaded the tapes. He traced one computer hard drive belonging to Louis Maxwell, Jr."

"But that's good news." Susan said excitedly not understanding why Griffin was sounding so alarmed. "What did he find? Anything about location?"

"There were files on there. Files on everyone who is close to Raven. Including you." Griffin informed her. "He knows about you. We heard everything that happened inside, in the back and in the parking lot meaning so did he. Jinx said this is best high tech technology he's never seen. You need to get over here."

Susan was already getting on her shoes. "Why aren't you sounding happy about this?"

"Jinx said with the security video system that was set up there should have been no way he could break into any of the computers or hard drives." Griffin informed her. "It was meant to be hacked."

"Okay, I'm on my way." Susan hung up and tried to call Raven. It went straight to voicemail. "Do you ever answer your fucking phone. I swear I'm starting to get a complex thinking you don't want to talk to me. I'm heading over to the compound. Get your ass over there unless you are already there then wait for me. I'm on my way." After that she didn't even try to call Lana, just sent her a quick text.

Grabbing her keys, she unlocked her backdoor and swung it open to see a man standing in the doorway. She screamed dropping her keys to reach for her gun.

"Hello, Susan." He said, his lips spreading into a smirk, her name sounding creepy as hell coming from his mouth. The last thing Susan thought was she was changing her name.

Raven drove her motorcycle up to the cemetery gates and got off. She pushed it to its usual spot then jumped the gate. Charger had to leave for his shift, which he was late for. She grinned remembering watching him from the window as he walked to the SUV then stood for a second staring at the windshield she had broken with the rock. He had shaken his head then glanced to where she was watching him, then grinned and gave her that sexy wink.

She had a few hours before she had to meet up with Lana and Susan, so she decided to head here instead of sitting at home alone. After Jake's words she knew she had to come. Raven was anxious to tell Tracy that she and Charger had mated. It was still fresh and hard to believe, but Raven had never felt happier and knew her friend would be happy for her also. Shaking the guilty feelings aside she put her phone on silent as she walked toward her friend's final resting place. Reaching out to touch the cool marble as she always did, she stopped. An envelope sat on the top with her name scribbled across it.

Scanning the area, she frowned as she picked up the white envelope. She wondered if it was maybe from Jake. Opening it she unfolded the paper and felt her whole life shift.

It's time, Raven. Time for this to end. I know you've finally figured out that it was me behind the Guardian explosion. I'm sorry about your friends, especially Tracy. Such a lovely girl.

Oh, wait. You're right, Raven. I'm not sorry at all.

I warned you. I promised you that I would take away all those you held dear just as you tried to take what I held dear. On the back is a map to where I will be, but I won't be alone. Bring everyone if you'd like, but only you can save the two closest to you. Be quick, Raven. Time is running out. It's time for you to choose who means the most to you. See you soon.

Regards,

Louis Maxwell, Jr.

Trying to remain calm she turned the paper over and looked on the back. She studied the map quickly and knew exactly where it was. She had been at the old airfield a few times in the past. A noise to her left had Raven dropping into defense mode. Jake walked around the corner. Surprise lit his face as he looked at her, then turned deadly as he saw her expression.

"What's wrong?" Jake asked looking down at the paper in her hand.

Without saying a word, she handed him the letter, then pulled out her phone. Seeing a missed call and voicemail she played it. Susan's voice came over the phone speaker. Raven glanced up at Jake who was now looking at the map on the back.

She hit Charger's name putting the phone on speaker. It began to ring and on the fourth ring it stopped. "Charger?" Raven said, but something told her that Charger wasn't on the other end. Static came over the speaker, then cut out and the line went dead. Her eyes met Jake's. She tried one more time and it was the same. Panic began to eat at her, but she ignored it.

"Where's my sword?" She asked Jake whose eyes had turned black with rage.

"Where it should be." Jake answered her with no further explanation.

Her phone rang and she answered right away without looking at it. "Charger?"

"No, it's Ryker." Ryker's voice sent disappointment through her. "Is Susan with you?"

"No." Her eyes once again met Jake's. She now knew who Louis had. "Meet Jake at the compound."

"The bar was wired with high tech security cameras." Ryker informed her. "Jinx hacked into the system. They saw and heard everything that was done and said inside and outside. I think he has Susan, Raven. She was supposed to be here at the compound, but never showed."

Raven closed her eyes tightly and cursed. "And Charger." She replied, her voice hard.

"Fuck!" Ryker cursed long and loud. "Motherfucker."

"Jake is on his way. Get everyone and I mean everyone at the compound. I want anyone who has dealt with Demons especially, and tell Steve, Ronan, and Bishop if they have a problem with it tough shit. I want Mira, Kira, and Bonnie. If they disagree, then you tell them if anything happens to Charger or Susan, I will kill them myself. Got it?"

"Got it." Ryker replied, then hung up the phone.

"I want you to get them together and meet me there." Raven was back in Guardian mode. This was Demon territory where she excelled. She would not fail. "The bastard wants a war, then let's give him a fucking war. No one and I mean no one fucks with a Dark Guardian."

"But you aren't a Dark Guardian anymore." Jake's eyes were still black as night as he threw that at her.

"Today I am." She responded then took off at a run trusting Jake to do exactly what she said. No way in hell was this bastard going to take anyone else away from her. Louis Maxwell was right about one thing, today this was going to end.

CHAPTER 23

*R*aven walked into the church, did the sign of the cross and made her way downstairs. Finding the bookcase, she pushed it aside as she punched in the code. The secret door opened immediately. Every Dark Guardian was a part of the religious community because of what they dealt with. It was seeped into their souls to protect God's children against the evils of Satan. No matter where she was in her life, that would always be a part of her...a part of any Dark Guardian.

Walking to the back of the room where the weapons of past Guardians were stored, she saw it. The sword was her choice of vengeance against the evil they as Dark Guardians faced. Sliding it out of its holder, she smiled. "Good to see you again, girl." Slipping the strap over her shoulder, she then went through a separate door.

Each weapon the Dark Guardians used was blessed and infused with Holy water. Kneeling down she placed the tip of her sword on the ground and then placed her forehead on the hilt of the weapon. Closing her eyes, she silently meditated for strength, guidance, and the foresight of the battle she was walking into. The tattoo of the Raven on her arm began to burn and tingle, as she felt the feathers tickle her skin. She knew it was time. Opening her eyes, she stood as light from an unseen force beamed down on her.

"I will not fail." Her voice was level with a definite tone filled with confidence. Turning she expertly slipped the long deadly blade into its sleeve on her back and walked out of the room, through the weapon room closing the door behind her. Pushing the bookcase back she saw a priest standing in the corner.

"Good to see you back." He whispered as he bowed his head. "God be with you."

Raven nodded then continued up the stairs and out of the church. Jumping on her bike she took off. Within minutes she pulled up to the place marked on the map. A swarm of Warriors and Guardians stood behind Jake. Stopping she glanced at the airplane hangar giving it a once over before stopping in front of everyone.

"I'm not expecting anyone here to fight Demons." She began her eyes searching each of them. Sloan stood to the side staring at her, but remained silent. "What I do expect is for—"

"Who the hell made you boss?" Sonya, who was just to her left, called out and before she even finished her last word Raven's sword point was at her throat.

"I did." Raven said calmly. "And if you don't like it leave. I don't care what you have against me, but we can settle it afterwards or if you keep running your fucking mouth I will kill you right now. I don't care. There is one of us in there as well as an innocent that is what I care about. Now are you finished?"

Sonya swallowed hard. "Yes."

Raven gave her one glare before she removed her blade from Sonya's throat. "Jill keep an eye on this bitch."

"You got it." Jill said more than happy to be assigned to that job.

She then looked at Mira, Kira, and Bonnie. "I know this is asking a lot, but I need you to shield as many of our people as possible as well as yourself. They are going to try to—"

"We got this, Raven." Bonnie said as Kira and Mira both nodded. "We know what we need to do. You just focus on what *you* need to do. This isn't my first rodeo with the bastards."

"He will kill them if any of us fight." Daniel informed her of something she already knew. How he knew this surprised her. Then again it was Daniel.

"I know." Raven said, then looked around again. The Guardians knew what she was about to say, but some of the Warriors were not accustomed to their ways or the Demon ways. "If I go down that is when and only when you attack. Do everything in your power to save Charger and Susan."

"Why can't we do that now?" Steve said not looking happy that Mira was on the frontlines.

"Because they will die instantly." Daniel responded for Raven.

"Fuck." Steve cursed looking more serious than Raven had ever seen him. She hated she was putting everyone at risk, but for Charger and Susan she would die just to save them both.

Her eyes caught Ryker glaring at the building. "Do I have to worry about you playing hero?"

His eyes shifted to her and narrowed. "Don't worry about me, just watch your own ass."

Raven nodded her gaze then met Kane's and then Jared's. He walked up to her and put his hand on her shoulder. "You got this, daughter."

"Yes, I do." Raven said confidently.

Jared gave her a nod, then turned toward everyone else. "Quick Demon checklist before all hell breaks loose. They smell like a week-old shit that sat in a toilet someone didn't flush."

Raven gave him a sideways glare. "Really, Jared. You start off with that?" One thing Raven had learned being with the Warriors is that they went into dangerous ass situations with a sense of humor.

"He's not lying." Bonnie snorted with a nod.

"See, Bonnie knows and I'm sure those with weak stomachs would like to know that information." Jared looked back to everyone else. "Weapons will be no good unless it's been infused with Holy water. Any weapon that can be used to cut their head off doesn't need to be infused. Just whack that sucker right off."

"In Damon's case just twist and snap it comes right off." Sid said with a half grin glancing over to where Damon stood with his crossed glaring at him.

"Just get behind Damon, folks." Jared said then turned serious. "How many, Kane?"

"Seventy-five." Kane answered, no smile on his face.

"Jake?" Jared eyes moved in his direction. "Same."

"I got eighty." Raven said without being asked. "But the fuckers look alike so I may have counted a few twice."

"I got eighty also." Bonnie said, then gave Raven a wink. "Told you it wasn't my first rodeo. I'm sure you know where there's eighty of these bastards, there's a hundred or so more."

"What the hell is going on?" Steve, who had been listening intently to Jared's little speech, frowned. "Do they smell like week-old shit or not?"

Raven actually grinned not taking her eyes off the airplane hangar and the demons filling the windows watching them. Fucking Steve.

"Yes, Steve. They smell like shit." Jared sighed with a grin. "Demons are also nosey and impatient as fuck. While I was giving you the run-down the Guardians were counting how many they could count so we have an ideal what we are walking into."

"They are also stupid as fuck." Kane added glaring at the hangar. "They are trying to figure out why we aren't making a move yet. The more impatient they get the more they are off their game. We use that to our advantage."

"Any questions?" Jared glanced at Steve who just shook his head, but then opened his mouth.

"Yeah." Steve said looking around. "Where's Damon. I want behind his big ass."

Chuckles filled the air releasing some of the tension. Raven moved her head back and forth getting ready for what was about to happen. She knew that nothing would happen to Charger or Susan while they stood outside. They were actually safer because as soon as Raven appeared that's when they would both be in danger. Louis wanted to watch her suffer so he wouldn't do anything until she appeared.

"Let's do this." Raven said, glancing at Jared who was now facing the hangar. She then looked to her other side where Jake walked beside her.

"Jake." Raven said as they began to walk as one. "This is for Tracy. Stay as close to me as possible."

"Wouldn't want to be anywhere else." Jake answered, his voice hard with vengeance.

Just as they were approaching the large hangar doors, she glanced at Ryker who without having to be told swept his hand out and the door exploded. The first thing she saw was Charger hanging up in the rafters, underneath him was a wooden makeshift platform of tall spikes. If he fell death would be certain. Her eyes followed the rope that hung toward a large platform that connected a lever.

"You see that?" She whispered to Jake, who grunted indicating he did.

She glanced at Susan who stood on the platform being held by a man who looked oddly familiar, he had eyes of a demon and yet. Something wasn't quite right. Finally, she let her eyes go to Charger who was staring at her and shaking his head. She had to look away. Any emotion she showed meant certain death for a lot of people.

"Stay back." She whispered to Bonnie who was on her other side. She walked forward her eyes scanning the area, forming a plan.

"Raven, don't you fucking do this." Charger growled down at her. "Don't you fucking dare! Jared get her the hell out of here."

"Yes, Raven." A voice that had haunted her for so long spoke. Her eyes searched another larger platform higher up to see Louis step out of the shadows. "Don't do it." He mocked Charger which enraged Charger.

Raven blocked it all out. "What do you want, Louis. Other than to make me suffer? I'm here. Let them go and do whatever you think you have to do to me."

"Now what fun is that?" Louis leaned over the rail to stare at her. She noticed he gave a hand single and without thought she pulled her sword. Swinging with all her might she felt her sword meet that of Demon flesh. The sounds of gurgling filled her ears. She didn't even look down at the dead, only up at Louis who didn't look happy. He hit the lever which sent Charger a few inches toward the ground. Her stomach rose to her throat, but she kept her fear hidden.

"I'm fucking bored already." Raven smirked up at him. "What game are you wanting to play, Louis."

"I knew you'd come around to my way of thinking." Louis took his hand off the lever. "If you beat my Demons, then you get to choose which one to save. Your lover or your new best friend. But I have to tell you this girl has caught the heart of my son."

"Your son?" Dammit, Raven let him see her shock.

"Oops, I let that slip didn't I." Louis laughed acting a little manic. "You see, Raven, I lied. My son didn't die after all. He's alive and well. My wife, the bitch, did die but not until after giving birth to this little demon. I kept her alive long enough, even after that terrible unfortunate fall you caused. I faked their deaths because I knew if the authorities saw what my wife was going to give birth to then they would have killed him. I couldn't have that."

"Sick fuck." She heard Jake mumble.

"Everything was planned. It was you that messed everything up and it's you that will pay. My wife was obedient until you." He screamed as he stabbed his finger toward her with so much hate Raven felt it. "I lost everything. My money, my Demons and it took me many years to acquire what you took from me, you bitch!"

She knew she had to get control and not let his crazy rant affect her for what was about to happen. "Yeah, well, congrats on the kid, I guess." Raven said glancing at the man holding onto to Susan. Now she knew why he looked so familiar. "Now about this game. When I win, I can only choose one person to save."

"If you win?" He laughed snapping his fingers. Demons came out of the shadows all glaring at her as if she was their next meal. "Sure, if you win then one can go free."

"Your contest sucks!" Raven spat on the ground as she glared up at him. "How about I kill your Demons as you call them, they both go free, and you die. That's *my* contest."

"Those are not the rules!" He screamed down at her and Raven knew she had gotten to him. It was too easy. She glanced back at Bonnie sending her a message and thank God she kept her mind open to hear it. She looked at Kane and did the same thing before turning back toward Louis. "They can't help you!"

"I know." Raven growled, then glanced at the Demons surrounding her. "Are you going to keep crying up there or are you going to send in your Demons, bitch."

"Raven no!" Charger bellowed, but Raven was past hearing him. It had begun and what was going to happen was going to happen, she just hoped she was good enough that Charger and Susan survived this.

The first wave came at her and Raven closed her mind to everything other than what needed to be done and that was kill as many of these fuckers as she could. She lost count of how many she had sliced, stabbed, kicked, headbutted and killed. They kept coming and she kept going. She took some hard hits, but nothing that stopped her. She was like a killing machine. It was what she had been trained to do, trained by the best.

Demons were not good fighters, but they could be deadly if you took them for granted. Two Demons tried to rush her, but she elbowed one in the face while stabbing the other one from behind before swinging her blade and cutting off the head of the one holding its nose. The stench was almost as overwhelming as the onslaught of Demons coming at her. Some of them were in human form, others were not. It didn't matter, they all died the same Demon death.

Suddenly it slowed enough for her to glance up to see Louis looking panicked. He was yelling at his son who was holding Susan. She saw him reach for the lever and screamed, "Now!"

Demons began to come at her again as she tried to watch Charger and Susan. Taking a hit that took her to her knees she spat blood.

"Knew you weren't nothing." The Demon hissed as he stood surrounded by dead Demons.

Raven swung around on her knees swinging her sword taking his legs right off. "Fuck you, dumbass." She hissed just as she heard the rope holding Charger break. Relief was swift when Kane dove knocking Charger clear of the spikes. Without hesitation she ran and jumped to the platform, her sword at Louis's throat.

"Let her go, or daddy gets it." Raven ordered his son who held Susan against him.

"No!" He shouted backing up, his black inhuman eyes glared at them. "She is mine."

"Max!" Louis cried out at his son's betrayal. "What are you doing? Help me. You promised not to let anything happen to me. Son, please!"

"I am not your son!" Max growled at him his black eyes glowed with hate. "I've been your slave you bastard."

"Guess it's not your day, Louis." Raven bent down close to his face. "But your death is not mine to collect."

Grabbing him by the throat she picked him up and looked over the rail. Her eyes instantly found Charger who was glaring up at her though in relief, but still glaring. Yeah, she was going to catch hell for this one. Spotting Jake she tossed Louis over the rail. "Jake." She called out just as Louis hit the ground then tried to get up and run. "He is not my kill to collect."

Jake gave her a nod, then stalked toward Louis. She turned away facing Max who was chanting something. "Max, let her go and we will let you live." Raven said, but he continued to chant.

Raven tried to give Susan a reassuring look, but noticed her eyes were glazed over. She headed that way, but Daniel grabbed her arm stopping her.

"What is he doing?" Raven frowned trying to get out of Daniel's grip. "Let me go. Susan!"

"Ryker!" Daniel yelled the urgency in his voice evident.

"Is he transporting her?" Raven started to fight, but Daniel wasn't giving in. "Dammit, let me fucking go."

Just as Ryker jumped over the rail his gaze landed on Susan with Max. Susan's eyes opened wide as she screamed Ryker's name.

Ryker jumped grabbing onto them both as all three disappeared into thin air.

"No!" Raven screamed just as Charger grabbed her from Daniel.

"I couldn't let her go." Daniel said to Charger. "Not where he's taking Susan."

"Where is he taking her?" Raven turned toward Daniel enraged. "Where is he fucking taking her, dammit?"

Daniel closed his swirling eyes for a second, then opened them again this time they were solid white. "Somewhere that only Ryker can save her."

"No." Raven raged then slammed her hands on the ground. "Fuck!"

Charger pulled her into his arms and held her. "He will get her, Raven." Charger said holding her so tight. "If anyone can save her it's Ryker."

Staring out over the hangar she saw that everyone was staring up at them. Her eyes shifted toward Jake who bowed his head toward her, the rest of the Guardians did the same. The Warriors thumped their chest as they also stared at her. She didn't deserve this show of respect. She had failed. Turning her head away from them she closed her eyes, but the vision she saw was the fear in Susan's eyes as she screamed Ryker's name.

CHAPTER 24

It had been a week since Susan and Ryker had disappeared and Raven was about to lose her shit. Sitting on Susan's picnic table she watched the chickens waddle around as if lost. Even that damn rooster Drumstick seemed depressed. He strutted over to her tilting his head sideways looking at her.

"Yeah, I know I miss her to." Raven whispered feeling her eyes welled up. Fuck, she felt so fucking helpless it was killing her. Wiping her eyes, she glanced at the garden. Someone had been coming and keeping up on the gardening, she didn't know who. She herself was coming by morning and night taking care of the chickens. She also got Susan's mail and put it inside.

Glancing up she saw Lana standing there staring at her. "Hey." Lana said as she walked over. "Guess the mystery of the chicken person has been solved."

Raven gave her a small smile. "Guess the secret gardener has been solved also."

Lana laughed, but her laughter quickly turned to sobs. Raven stood and held her close. Together they cried standing in Susan's backyard among the things Susan loved most. Her chickens and garden.

"I'm sorry." Raven swallowed hard. "I should have—"

"Don't you fucking dare blame yourself." Lana pulled away. "Susan would kick your ass if she heard you and I swear when she gets back, I will tell her. She will never let you live it down. She will drive you crazy."

"I just feel so fucking helpless." Raven hissed in frustration.

"Bonnie, Mira, and Kira are trying to reach Ryker. There is a way, but so far, they haven't been able to." Lana said giving her hope. "Sometimes they said it can take a while depending on where they are. Daniel is even trying. I'm not sure what he is able to do, but the guy is trying his best. He also feels responsible in some way."

"Ryker will find her." Raven said, then frowned. "I just hope it's soon."

They sat together in silence. The whole situation was so fucked up. It was well known that some people used Demons to impregnant humans. It was a sick practice, but it happened. Just like vampires trafficked humans to turn them into vampires for blood. It was just a fucking messed up world. Louis's wife never said a word to her about being impregnated by a Demon, had she even known, or had Louis been lying and Max wasn't his true son. Max had admitted as much, but he could have just been saying that out of hatred for his father.

"You're going to drive yourself crazy." Lana glanced over at her. "Believe me, I know."

Before she could respond Charger and Sid walked into the backyard followed by Daniel. "What are you guys doing here?" Lana frowned.

"We've been stopping by checking on Susan's place. Some of us just left Ryker's and decided to meet up here." Sid said, then pulled her into his arms.

Daniel walked up to Raven. "You forgive me?"

Raven nodded, then reached out and hugged Daniel. "There's nothing to forgive, Daniel."

Soon Susan's backyard was filled with Warriors, Mates and Guardians. A few of the guys, Charger included reinforced the chicken house to make sure nothing that didn't belong could get inside. Raven sat back watching, then smiled when Charger came up and gave her a hug and kiss on the forehead.

"Susan would be in heaven right now." Lana said as tears streamed down her face. "She always wanted company and now look."

Nodding Raven kept her tears in check because she had been thinking the same thing. She smiled up at Charger who was staring down at her. He had scolded her ass hard for what she had done that day to save him, but she would do it all over again without hesitation. He had also told her how damn proud he had been of her skills. Then proceeded to teasingly take credit for those Demon killing skills.

"I love you." She whispered in his ear.

"And I love you." He whispered back with a tight hug. "He will find her and bring her back, Raven."

She nodded, but the longer it went the more doubts she had. Every Guardian knew that humans who were trapped in the Demon realm usually didn't survive long without losing their minds. That was the fear she had for Susan.

~

Raven walked into the compound; her mind busy on what needed to be done for the day. Glancing toward Sloan's office she bypassed it and headed to the kitchen. Going inside she spotted Daniel standing against the sink eating a bowl of cereal.

His eyes rose to stare at her. "It won't work."

"Why the hell not?" Raven said, then frowned. "And stop doing that. It creeps me out. Let me ask my question before you answer it."

"Okay, but it still won't work." Daniel grinned with a shrug.

"Dammit." Raven bit her nail. "You mean it won't work because it won't work, or it won't work because you don't think Charger will allow it?"

"Both." Daniel said after he thought about it for a minute. "Listen, it's been too long. If you went in now, you wouldn't even know where to go. Ryker went with them. There's a big difference."

"You could lead me." Raven cocked her eyebrow at him. "I know you have skills that only you know about Daniel. Come on, it can work."

"It won't work." Daniel annoyingly repeated.

"Shit." Raven cursed then tried once more. "Will you help me if I do it anyway?"

"It won't work." This time that didn't come from Daniel, but Bonnie who stood behind her.

"Told ya." Daniel said, then put his bowl in the sink. "Give Ryker time."

Raven glared at Daniel as he walked out of the kitchen. She then turned to Bonnie. "Anything yet?"

"No," Bonnie shook her head. "But I may know someone who can help us. I've got a call in. Just give me time and let me see what I can do."

"Bonnie, she may not have much time left." Raven said, but then nodded. "But okay, anything is better than nothing."

"Exactly." Bonnie gave her a wave as she headed out. "I'll keep in touch, Rave."

Hearing the nickname Susan called her hit Raven hard. Falling back against the counter she put her head in her hands and lost it.

"Hey." Sloan's voice startled her.

"I just need a minute." Raven turned trying to hide her face. Huge hands grasp her shoulders turning her around just as they wrapped around her in a comfortable, almost fatherly hug. Holy crap Sloan was comforting her, and she was allowing it. She must really be losing it.

"I've only told one person this before and I swear I will deny ever saying it." Sloan whispered. "But if I ever had a daughter,

I would want her to be like you and Jill mixed together. To watch what you did in that hangar was something I will never witness again. Your loyalty to those close to you is priceless."

"Thank you." She nodded against his chest, then he pulled away and forced her to look up at him.

"Never blame yourself for what happened." Sloan glared down at her. "I've known Ryker for a long time. If anyone can bring Susan back it's him, Raven. To show you how much faith I have in him...if he doesn't bring her back, I will step down from my position."

"That's saying a lot, Sloan...wait a minute." Raven glared up at him in a teasing manner. "Jared has told me you mention stepping down almost every week."

Sloan grinned with a wink, but then turned serious. "Ryker will be back with Susan." He turned to walk away, but stopped when she called his name.

"You really do like me, don't you?" Raven said spotting Charger standing just inside the door.

"You're a pain in my ass." Sloan said, then gave Charger a nod before exiting.

Charger walked up to her with a cocked eyebrow. "Am I going to have to kick Sloan's ass? Was he just hugging you?"

Raven snorted shaking her head. "Sloan hug me?" She chuckled, then wrapped her arms around him laying her head on his chest. Her eyes looking at where Sloan had disappeared. Out of everything she had been told or assured of Susan's disappearance, Sloan's words made her believe that maybe...just maybe Susan had a chance. "Never."

Pulling away from Charger she looked up at him. "I need to go see Tracy."

"Come on." Charger wrapped his arm around her leading her out of the kitchen. "It's been a while since I've visited."

Raven smiled as they made their way past Sloan's office. She glanced inside to see Sloan behind his desk talking on the phone. He looked her way giving her a nod before going back to his conversation. She was definitely seeing Sloan Murphy in a whole different light.

Climbing on Charger's bike she wrapped her arms around him. Riding on the back of Charger's motorcycle was something she would always love. It wasn't long before they were pulling into the cemetery. Being there during regular hours was different for Raven. She hardly was ever here when it was open. They drove down the small road that ended at her gravesite.

Getting off she walked that way happy not to see a letter on the top. She laid her hand on the cool marble. "Sorry, it's been a while Trace." Raven said with a small smile. "Thanks for not haunting me."

Charger walked behind her and wrapped his arms around her waist, his chin resting on the top of her head. "Do you think Tracy would have been happy that we're mated?"

"She always said we would be one day." Raven said, then chuckled. "I never believed her though."

"She always told me the same thing." Jake's voice had them both looking that way.

"Are you always here?" Raven smiled at him, then accepted his hug.

"Not as much lately." Jake said, clasping Charger on the shoulder. "Any word on Susan or Ryker?"

"No, nothing." Raven sighed sinking deeper back into Charger's body.

"Raven thank you for what you did that day." Jake said after a few minutes of silence. "You had every right…"

"No, I didn't." Raven stopped him. "It was your right to take the life that took Tracy. Not mine."

Jake nodded, then touched the marble like Raven always did. "She would have been damn proud of you that day, Raven. She loved you like a sister."

Raven nodded with a sad smile. "I miss her so much Jake."

"Yeah." Jake said, then turned away. "I'll see you guys later."

Once he was gone Raven turned into Charger. "Do you think he will ever be okay?"

"If it had been you, I know I wouldn't be. You have been and are my life." Charger lifted her face and kissed her. "That's how much I love you, Raven."

A red bird landed on the white marble and chirped loudly. Both Raven and Charger watched as it continued singing away as it stared at them.

"Do you think that's Tracy giving us her blessing?" Charger grinned watching the beautiful bird.

"I know it is." Raven said also watching it. Her happiness dimmed slightly as her thoughts went back to Susan. Would their world ever be safe? Knowing the answer to that she hugged Charger even tighter hoping she wouldn't have two gravestones to visit.

Printed in Great Britain
by Amazon